Dragonfly

By Leigh Talbert Moore

Dragonfly
Copyright © Leigh Talbert Moore, 2013
www.leightmoore.com
Printed in the United States of America.

Cover design by Jolene B. Perry.

*To my friends in Baldwin County and to the
Alabama Gulf Coast,
which inspired this story.*

Chapter 1

The first time I saw the Gulf of Mexico I didn't believe it was real.

The colors were so vivid – turquoise and deep marine blue splashing on sparkling-white grains of sand – it was as if the whole place glowed in the sunlight. It was beautiful. Magical.

I had no idea it would change my life. That my parents' decision to move our family almost a thousand miles south, to their tiny hometown just off the coast, would drop me into the middle of a decades-old impasse.

A separation mandated by a long-forgotten crime.

A secret I would accidentally revive.

* * *

Last day of summer break. I was alone at the public beach just south of Fairview, my new hometown, feeling sorry for myself. Senior year was a day away, and Gabi, the best friend I'd made since we moved here, was gone, her Coast Guard dad reassigned to Key West.

A military brat, Gabi was practiced at the art of breaking into a new town, meeting a whole new group of people. I was preparing for the loneliest year of my life.

We'd lived in Fairview three years, and I still didn't get southern "hospitality." People weren't *weird* here, they were *quirky* or *eccentric*. On top of that, everybody knew everybody, and if you didn't ask about everyone's family members, most importantly their mothers, you were considered rude.

It was a setup I was destined to fail, but Gabi could always turn it around with a funny quip or a hilarious questioning of how anyone could be so nice. They were clearly either hiding a secret life or they needed to get one. Now I was the one entering senior year in need of a life. Of course, I had other friends, but none like Gabi. We shared everything, and now it was just me and my journal.

On the beach, I could pretend it wasn't happening. I could close my eyes behind giant shades, and disappear into the sounds of Nova Bossa, which my earbuds delivered directly to my brain. My crazy-curls were tied in a knot at the base of my neck under a huge, Audrey Hepburn-style straw hat, and I pretended I was somebody important, tanning outside of Cannes or Nice. Maybe a cabana boy would bring me a fruity drink, and I would call someone *darling* or something unexpected like that.

I was no longer Anna, the outsider. I was a star.

The song ended, my damp eyes flickered open, and there they were — right next to me on the sand, facing the opposite direction. Not really setting up camp or even looking like they planned to stay for long. Just glowing in the sun.

"Dad will never go for this, Lucy," the guy said.

He was incredible. Tanned, slim, and somewhere around my age — maybe a little older. His blonde hair blew in his eyes, which I couldn't see behind his dark Ray-Bans, and he moved in a way that radiated confidence. He was the type of guy I was sure got whatever he wanted. I slid my filmy beach-wrap across my soft stomach, wishing I did more sit-ups and thankful at least my frizz was well-hidden.

Lucy's hair was perfect. It was the exact same color as his and hung down her back. It blew in beachy waves around her arms, and she slid one thick lock behind her shoulder before turning to touch my arm. I jumped as if I'd been electrocuted.

"Excuse me," she said, smiling like a Junior Miss contestant. "Have you been here all day?"

"Um... no," I said, cheeks hot. "I've only been here about an hour."

"Oh, sorry. I was just looking for someone. I thought you might've seen him. I'm Lucy, by the way."

"Anna," I said, shaking the hand she offered. "And I didn't. Sorry."

"No worries, Anna." She was still smiling as she turned away again.

I was sure I'd seen her red bikini on television, and she had the supermodel body to wear it. For a moment I wondered if they might be as-yet unknown celebrities, here for a secret, incognito weekend before going public and becoming superstars. Only, why would they pick this spot?

More likely they were from Crystal Beach or Hammond Island—one of the ritzy gated communities lining the coast to the east. Only, it still didn't make sense for them to be here. Those places had their own guarded beaches, safe from the commoners like me.

The guy spoke again in his smooth, deep voice. "Let's go. He's not coming."

"You're being annoying, Jack," she said, leaning back on her elbows and getting comfortable. "It's only been five minutes. He hasn't had a chance."

"I can't believe you're doing this again."

She waved at the turquoise water. "Cool off and give him a few more minutes."

It was impossible not to stare as Jack walked down to the shore. His unbuttoned shirt blew in the breeze showing off his lined torso, and his board shorts hung

7

loosely around his waist. The water rushed around his legs and my heart beat a little faster as I imagined the impossible — me standing beside him, him putting his arm around me, maybe pulling me in for a hug. I actually shivered at the thought.

I didn't have a ton of experience with guys, but I knew what a hug felt like. And in a place where most people lived in swimsuits half the year, I was familiar with the sensation of skin against skin.

Suddenly he turned back. I squeezed my eyes shut, embarrassed, even though I knew he couldn't see me watching him behind my dark sunglasses. When I peeked again, he was back on the towel, feet shoved in the sand, seeming angry.

"So is B.J. short for 'bad joke'?"

Lucy shook her golden hair back. "Something must've happened."

"Good. This was a setup for trouble. Again."

"I don't know what you're talking about."

"You do," Jack said. "And it won't get you what you want."

She sat up and smiled, blinking innocently. "I want to find the cute lifeguard I met at Scoops yesterday."

"You want things to be different with Dad." Jack's voice was low and even.

"Dad can go straight to hell."

"Yes, that's exactly the message you send."

Jack exhaled and smoothed the sand under his hands. I was flat-out eavesdropping, no getting around it, but their conversation fascinated me. Not to mention, he was in perfect view.

"Besides," Lucy sighed, her voice a little sad. "I can't change the reason Dad hates me."

"He doesn't hate you —"

"Or pretends I don't exist." She slid her long hair back and held it in a ponytail for a moment before dropping it. "But you know what? I'm glad I look like Mom. She was a beauty queen. You got a few of her genes yourself."

Jack stood and grabbed his towel. "This conversation is stupid. And I'm leaving."

"Whatever. It's hot." She pulled her long cover-up over her head, and hot or not, she looked fresh, like she hadn't been in the sun at all.

My eyes followed them back to the parking lot where Jack threw their stuff into the back of steel-grey Jeep. Two doors slammed and they sped off, heading east, in the direction of Hammond Island. And that, I assumed, was the end of it.

For a few moments, everything felt quieter. Even the sun seemed a bit dimmer with their departure. I stood and walked to the water's edge. The smell of salt and fresh fish always hung in the air here, and sometimes dolphins could be spotted swimming around, playing just off the coastline. If I were going to be abandoned, at least it was in a pretty place. The noise of the breaking waves comforted me, and I pulled off my hat so my light-brown hair could blow free. It would be huge and horrible in less than ten seconds, but I didn't care.

The further east you traveled, along the Florida coastline, the water grew more and more turquoise, the sand more sugary-white. Maybe for my next escape I'd drive to Nana's place in Navarre and spend the night. Today I'd just wanted to be alone.

I had a plan for the year, at least. With my new position reporting for the school newsblog, my college applications were set. SAT scores would be in soon, and hopefully by this time next year I'd be entering Northwestern, the top journalism school in the country.

That just left 365 days to endure.

I exhaled, and as I stood staring far out at the horizon, I wished something exciting would happen to me. Just once. Something to take my mind off the monotony or at least make my life a little more interesting.

No chance of that in this tiny town of less than ten thousand full-time residents.

A lifeguard had arrived when I walked back to gather my stuff. All the public beaches had them, and they were usually savage-tanned college guys perched in the tall-wooden booths under the beach warning flags. Yellow today. Moderate hazard.

I watched him scan the sunbathers. He was dark with a perfect body—a requirement for life guarding here, it seemed. At this time of year he had to be a local, but I didn't know him.

"Hey," I called up.

He looked down at me, eyebrows pulled together. "Whatcha need, kid?"

Some joke. He couldn't have been more than nineteen, and I'd be eighteen in a few months.

"Are you B.J.?"

"Who wants to know?"

"A girl..." I started, and then wondered what I was even doing. "I just thought I recognized you."

He looked at me like I'd had too much sun. Maybe I had. I shrugged and walked away, thinking they should've waited. Not that it mattered to me.

Beach escape had ended. It was time to face my life back on shore.

Chapter 2

Fairview High School had about six hundred students total, and as I stood observing my fellow seniors squealing and embracing each other, again I felt the sting of loneliness. Not having Gabi here was like watching one of those rock band reunions without the original lead singer. Just wrong.

Rachel, a friend of Gabi's who I'd sat behind last year in English, broke through my quiet despair, calling my name as she hurried to catch up with me. She wore a blue and white cheerleader uniform, and her perfectly straight blonde hair was smoothed back with a yellow grosgrain ribbon for a headband.

"You missed Open House Friday," she said, perky as always.

"Yeah, I thought I had a stomach bug or something."

It was a lie. I'd spent Friday drowning my depression in Chex Mix and root beer while I watched *The Notebook* for the thousandth time. Only it was first time without my best friend. Yep, pretty pathetic.

"Oh!" She jumped back almost a foot. "Were you puking or what?"

"I just had cramps. Maybe it was PMS?"

"Thank goodness!" She sighed dramatically. Then she bumped my arm. "Heard you made the school newsblog. Awesome."

"Yeah," I said, thinking how Rachel was a notorious gossip. "You should've tried out."

"Ha! As if I have time for that." She pushed her perfect hair behind her shoulder.

"Besides, I can't write worth a flip," she finished.

"Oh, well, I was just thinking how you always have the scoop."

I liked Rachel, we just had nothing in common. In addition to being head cheerleader, she'd dated her boyfriend Brad Brennan since middle school. Brad was the star of our high school football team, the Dolphins. Clichés had to start somewhere I guessed.

"Show me your schedule," Rachel said, breaking my thoughts. She quickly scanned our class listings. "Hmm… no matches. But we have the same lunch period. See you then?"

"Okay," I said, thinking how even though our future plans were vastly different, Rachel was still pretty decent, unlike some of the other cheerleaders. We might never be soul sisters, but she was at least a friend.

I ducked into English class, happy for the escape. I loved to read, and writing was my passion. Being tapped for the school newsblog was the icing on the cake, and I hoped it would make the time pass quickly.

My literature book was halfway out of my bag when I glanced up and almost dropped it on the floor. There he was. Again. Jack was standing in the doorway, totally hot and completely out of place in our required uniform khaki pants and white oxford shirt. I could swear he was still glowing. I couldn't breathe.

I closed my mouth and tried not to stare as he made his way to the seat next to mine. *What was he doing here?*

Mrs. Bowman walked in and everyone got quiet. "Welcome back, students. I expect you to be in your seats with your mouths closed," she said in her military monotone.

As she went down the list, I knew all the names from last year. We'd had to test to get in this class, and

"Why not? We can take Daddy's boat and cruise around when we need a break. Go lifeguard spotting." She winked, and I thought of B.J. How she'd just missed him, and how he'd called me *kid*. Ugh.

I was pretty certain I couldn't pull off lifeguard spotting. Or boats. And I wasn't even sure how to get onto Hammond Island. It seemed like I'd heard they had armed security guards at the entrance.

"I don't know," I said. "I kind of have this thing…"

"Just think about it. Bye, Anna!" She waved as the Jeep sped off.

How could I ever be friends with someone like Lucy Kyser? I didn't even know where to start trying to talk to her. But if I did, that would mean I might see Jack more. The very thought made my insides all squirmy. As if he'd even notice me.

Nope. Shying away was last-year's Anna. I was a school reporter now, and I was determined to be different. This could be an opportunity to do something interesting, and I certainly had a great excuse to try. Maybe I could do a feature story on notable new students. Who had hot twin brothers.

"You know those guys?" That friendly male voice put me at ease even though it sent most girls' hearts racing as fast as Jack Kyser's did.

That Kyser golden boy might've been the hottest new thing on campus, but Julian LaSalle was the reigning champ. An artist with dark hair and crazy blue eyes, Julian transformed black uniform pants (our other option) and a white oxford shirt into the epitome of post-punk chic with his tall, skinny swagger. Gabi and I had swooned since day one.

Gabi was also one of the reasons my Julian fantasies never took flight. The other was Renee Barron, the hottest girl in our class—before Lucy, of course. Julian was a notorious flirt, but when he did need a date, Renee always won that prized spot. And pending Renee's disappearance, Gabi had declared Julian hers. It was all in theory, of course, but it was still dibs.

Somehow, the removal of any chance of us ever getting together, regardless of how microscopic that chance might've ever been, had paved the way for us to become great friends. It was kind of cool. Except for the nerdy part where I was a Mathlete and assigned to tutor him in algebra last year. Still, a hot guy who was hopeless at math was too cute to be intimidating, and I could secretly fantasize about him all I wanted.

"Julian LaSalle," I tried to act coy, despite the smile spreading across my cheeks. "I heard you failed algebra even with all my efforts to save you."

He shrugged, clear blue eyes flirting behind his dark bangs. "It's all good. Just means we get to spend another year together."

"Sorry." I shook my head. "I quit the Mathletes. Reporting for the school newsblog instead."

"Motherf—what? What does that mean?" He actually looked mad. I wasn't sure how to take that.

I exhaled a laugh. "You're mad? I should be mad, since your failure made me look like a crap tutor. If it weren't for Allyson—"

"Allyson could focus." He smiled, throwing an arm across my shoulders. "I was too distracted by your brilliant mind." Then he caught one of my spiral locks the humid breeze blew straight in his face. "And these."

"Ugh," I grabbed all my frizz in a knot at my neck. "The worst."

"I love it. Titian. Venus of Urbino." He leaned his head to mine. "Renaissance women are hot."

"Are you saying I'm fat?"

He laughed. "You'll have to eat more pizza." Then he glanced back, over our shoulders and down. "Your little ass is still too cute for Botticelli."

Embarrassment squeezed my chest. "I'm not sure I agree with you." Then I shrugged off his arm. "Where's Renee?"

"She's around somewhere." He watched as I unlocked my car door and threw my bag on the passenger seat. "So you're making new friends?"

I shut the door and leaned against it. "I met Lucy at the beach Saturday. Sort of. And now I have classes with both of them. Jack doesn't say much... I'm sure he doesn't remember me."

"Doubtful. You are unforgettable, Anna Sunshine."

My brow relaxed. He knew I loved that nickname much better than my dad's horrifying "Anna Banana." I tried to imagine what Julian would say if I suggested we go out... If only I could be sure. Nothing would be more humiliating than me being serious while he was only playing.

"So what's this newsblog thing?" he said, straightening up.

"Features stuff. Interesting students, school events." My eyes widened. "Hey! I've got to do a story on you! You know, your art? It could be very serious, about your passion and your imagination..."

I was sure I sounded like a goose brainstorming, but Julian stepped closer. "Maybe a little demonstration," he said. "Some passion in my studio? Imagine it..."

A honk of nervous laughter came from my nose. "Oh, god," I muttered, cheeks blazing.

He laughed. "What? Too fast for the news?"

I cleared my throat, trying to find cool. "Actually, I would like to visit your studio. For the feature. I think you'd make a great subject."

"Mutual," he said, then caught my hand. "Check this out. See what you think."

He pulled up his shirt, and I struggled to breathe normally. Julian's body was legendary. Tanned from surfing all summer, lined and lean from lifting the heavy scrap metal he used for his sculptures, the fabric rose higher, and my head grew lighter until I saw it. A swirl of black lines formed a circular tattoo on his upper left ribcage. Nerves forgotten, I leaned in closer. It was still pink around the edges, and I saw it was his initials.

"Who did it?" I asked, carefully touching the strong, bold lines.

His skin flinched. "Did it myself."

My mouth fell open and I straightened, meeting his eyes. "You did not... did it hurt?"

He groaned, "Like a mother. Swiped a gun from Boze, then I had to call and confess. This part bled a lot, and I didn't know what to do."

I leaned down again, studying the very red outer edge.

"I think I went too deep." He dropped the shirt, and I stood. "He threatened to turn me in, of course, but I think he was impressed."

"It's pretty cool."

"And I can show you what else I'm working on. Machine parts as body parts. A foot-long spud wrench for a shin, a fender for the head, or more like a helmet." His enthusiasm was contagious. "And I've got an old V-twin motor I'm using for a pelvis."

"I love it! You could be my first story, and maybe I could take pictures to go with it."

"I'll take my shirt off." He pointed to his side. "This might be my new logo."

"I'm sure topless photos aren't allowed."

"I'm a guy." He said, as if that wasn't super-obvious. "Or whatever. Maybe I could just pick you up sometime, and we could do something."

Everything paused. *Was it possible Julian just asked me out?* Words escaped me.

He shrugged, backing away. "I mean, whatever. It was just a thought. See ya around, Anna."

Wait, what just happened? Julian never messed with my head like that. But Gabi was gone, so it wasn't like she could still call dibs. That only left the other reason, and Renee was apparently just "around somewhere."

He waved and trotted off, leaving me with two ideas buzzing in my brain. This year was starting off better than I expected.

Chapter 3

Story assignments were in, and I had successfully pitched my Julian feature. He'd agreed to email shots of his art to me, but I still hoped to visit his studio in their converted garage. The topic of Jack was another matter altogether. I hadn't even mentioned my notable students idea, as I was sure I'd never muster the nerve to speak to him.

Yes, we had English together, but every time I sneaked a peek, he was usually studying a book or writing something. Good thing because his blue eyes were absolutely hypnotic. The one time I sucked up the nerve to say hello, he looked straight at me, and my foot caught a chair leg. I nearly hit the floor, and I turned away fast, sliding into my seat, cheeks blazing. After that doofus move, I decided to focus on Lucy, who was a good student as I suspected. Still, she kept mentioning our need for a study-date, and after a series of texts, I caved.

That's how I found myself driving alone down the narrow, two-lane road to the gated entrance of Hammond Island. Maybe we could study, maybe we could talk about other things. But when I pulled into the driveway and saw just how huge their beige stucco mansion was, I almost turned the car around. My wardrobe was not prepared for this. And I wasn't so sure about my etiquette.

I shook my head. If I was going to be a real newswoman, I'd have to get over my inclination to be a chicken. For several moments, I sat in Mom's Kia doing my best to channel Martha Raddatz, Barbara Walters,

Christiane Amanpour, and all the other great newswomen who regularly chatted up the rich and powerful. This was my chance to join their ranks.

Bolstering my confidence, I approached the side entrance, planning how I might bring up the idea of a feature story. Until Jack opened the door, blue eyes and all. I jumped two feet.

"It's you!" I whispered.

He suppressed a grin. "You were expecting...?"

I did not say that I expected a servant to answer the door or that he looked amazing standing there in only a pair of running shorts and shoes. I couldn't look at his face again, but everywhere else I looked was just as disorienting.

"Lucy and I are supposed to be working on a project for school," I said.

"Sure, come on in." He stepped back and into the house. I followed him to a massive, beige stone and stainless kitchen and dining area. "I guess she thought you'd take longer. She went to the Tom Thumb. I was just going to run, but I can wait with you."

"Oh, no, I don't want to mess up your run." I really needed a mirror to be sure my curls weren't all frizzed or bunching up in their usual, freakish way.

"Nobody else is here," Jack smiled. I melted.

"Oh," I managed to say.

My professionalism was out the window, and I didn't dare bring up the story idea. We stood quietly for a bit, me trying to find anything to say, but all I could come up with was "You're super-hot," and who said that? I wished I'd read some of those sexiest man alive features. What would a professional say to him? I looked down at the stone floor. The huge room we stood in opened to another, larger living area.

"We have English class together," he finally said.

"Right! Mrs. Bowman. She's really tough, but I like her."

"You like to write," he smiled. I swooned again.

"How... how did you know that?"

"Every day you come in class and go straight to your journal. It's like you're in your own world."

"I guess I'm a nerd," I tried to laugh. *How embarrassing!*

"I always wonder what you're writing about." He leaned toward me on the bar, and my brain spun. I felt like I was having an out of body experience. He was leaning in, talking to me. I had to go with this.

"You do?" I asked.

"Yeah, like what did you write about today?"

"I can't remember..." My mind truly was blank. "The book we're reading? I love all our assignments for the semester."

His mouth curled down. "I don't like *Song of Solomon*."

"What? Toni Morrison's brilliant!"

"I don't like it. The story's... It's hard to read."

"Well, yeah, some of the scenes are pretty awful. But in the end, when Milkman flies, he's finally free. And the way she describes it, it's beautiful. But sad. I mean, when you compare it to the beginning, the suicide and all. It's like, only in death..." I stopped blabbering nonstop when I realized he was studying me, like he was curious about something. My nerves were back. I tried a different topic.

"Did Lucy ever find B.J.?" I said, remembering that first day on the beach, planning to say they'd just missed him.

"Who?" He straightened a card on the bar, his perfect brow lined. "Oh. I'd forgotten about that. No, she's into some brainiac she saw headed into the career center now."

"That's where the welding class meets." B.J. forgotten, I thought how Julian did some of his metal arts in the shop building. Since he was applying to the design college in Savannah, our administration let him invent his own electives, which made total sense because he was an artistic genius. "Some nice guys take classes in the career center."

"I just meant... Lucy likes to find ways to annoy our dad. That's all. So your boyfriend takes shop?" He smiled at me, and I didn't care about Lucy or shop guys or any of it.

"I don't have a boyfriend," I said.

Jack paused for a beat and looked at me as if he wanted to say more, but instead he turned to leave.

"I gotta go," he said. "Lucy should be back any minute."

I stared at the door after he closed it, and for a tiny moment, I let myself imagine walking around school holding hands with Jack Kyser. I'd be like Cinderella, and just look at his palace. My heart ticked faster and a little charge filled my middle. It was the stupidest dream, but it would be so... incredible.

Lucy jolted me back to reality, banging through the door, bags of snacks in hand. "Anna!" She looked fresh and pretty as always. "You beat me. I hope Jack kept you company until I got here. I saw him leave."

"Yeah, we talked about English class." I remembered what he said about watching me write and my heart did a little flip.

"Think he's cute?" She plopped the bags on the bar, a sneaky look on her face. "I could get him to ask you out. Maybe the Back to School dance Friday?"

My face went red. "Do not. I'd look like a total loser!"

"Leave it to me. I can be *very* subtle. And persuasive," she grinned and pulled out chips and dip. "He loves smart girls. And anyway, he needs to have some fun. Daddy's little over-achiever thinks way too much about the family business."

My lips twitched with all the questions that comment provoked. I considered bringing up the feature story again, but now I wasn't sure I wanted to mix business with what could be life-changing pleasure. Instead I took a chip and broke it into small pieces, trying to appear confident. "How can he not have a girlfriend? That's totally bizarre."

Lucy shrugged. "He's been out of the loop since Casey moved to college."

"Casey...?"

"Casey Simpson. Her parents live down the road in the red stone house with the big glass sunroom. You saw it?" I shook my head no. "She went to Vandy last year, but she and Jack were exclusive before that."

"Is she smart?" Confidence faltering.

"Oh, hells yeah. Pre-med, although I think she should've gone to Duke. But she wanted to be in Nashville. Good singer. Broke little Jackie-boy's heart."

That did it. I dropped the chip bits and dusted my fingers. I could not compete with that. I pulled out my books, ready to change the subject.

"So? You want to date my hot brother?" Lucy was getting excited again, and I could tell she wasn't going to stop.

"No. Thanks, but no."

"Why not?" she laughed.

"My parents would want to meet him, and… it's not a good idea." Besides my obvious inability to rank anywhere near this Casey Simpson person, I imagined my dad whipping out his Banana nickname and shuddered.

"Oh, please." Lucy's eyes rolled as she shook her head. "Your parents would love Jack. *Everyone* loves Jack."

"We'd better just stick to government." And reality.

"Sure. But if you change your mind…" Her sing-song voice trailed off as she turned to get a drink out of the refrigerator.

We worked until dark, and I headed out to Mom's car alone. It looked pretty ratty next to a gorgeous silver Audi that hadn't been here when I'd arrived. I didn't see Mr. Kyser enter the house, but I did see Jack sitting on the low stone wall that lined the driveway. He was slightly damp and absolutely perfect. Shirtless, his muscular shoulders glistened in the moonlight. My heart was racing, but I couldn't stop myself. I had to speak.

"Long run?" I sounded nervous, so I cleared my throat and pulled out my keys, hoping he didn't notice.

"Not really," he looked down. "I went for a swim while I was out."

"Isn't that dangerous? I mean, don't they say you could like… get eaten by a shark swimming at dusk?"

He let out a short laugh. "That would be random. But I'm used to sharks."

A frown creased my brow. "What do you mean?"

He looked away. "Ah, nothing. It's just so hot still. I wanted to cool off."

I studied his lips, wondering what it would feel like if they touched me. The thought made me shiver in the warm night air. I was hopeless. Squeezing my eyes shut against the humiliation, I blurted it out.

"Hey, listen. If Lucy says something to you about asking me out or anything, please just ignore her. I did *not* tell her to do that."

"What?" Those blue eyes met my hazel ones.

"Oh, god," I exhaled. "Lucy said something about talking to you, and I didn't want you to think I'd told her to do that."

Exit stage right; immediately die.

"Lucy wants to set us up?" He smiled, and I tried to imagine how beautiful their mother must've been to produce such perfect children.

"I guess," I said, looking down.

He got up and walked over to me. "I'm game. Go with me to that thing at school Friday."

"The dance?" I couldn't breathe. "Are you serious?"

He nodded, but in the same breath it was like he remembered something. "I mean, I don't know," he hesitated. "You're right. It's probably not a good idea."

"Wait... I didn't say that."

"It's just. My family can be difficult," he said. "And I'm kind of... well, I'm not really sure what's coming."

"Is anybody?" I tried to laugh, to lighten the mood, and for god's sake, save my date with him. "Lucy's not difficult."

Just then I heard the clink of ice on crystal. We both looked quickly as a dark figure emerged from the side patio and slowly walked in our direction. Jack straightened, stepping back.

"John?" a sharp voice said. I saw what could only be Bill Kyser step into the light. He was tall and slim with light brown hair and the same blue eyes as the twins. Only his eyes were cold and distant.

"Dad." Jack's casual manner was gone, and now he seemed tense. It made my hands shake as I fumbled with my keys.

"Who's your pretty friend?" Mr. Kyser smiled, but it was not welcoming. I needed to go.

"This is Anna Sanders. From school," Jack explained. "Lucy invited her over to work on a civics project."

"Sanders... Sanders..." Mr. Kyser frowned, his eyes surveyed my appearance. Then he switched gears, rocking his tumbler to the side. "Do you drink, Anna?"

"Dad." Jack said low.

"No, sir," I said.

"What type of birth control do you use?"

Heat filled my face. Jack shouted, "Dad! You're drunk, and Anna's going home."

I managed to get the car door open, despite my shaking hands. My vision was blurry, but it seemed Mr. Kyser chuckled as he took another drink and sauntered off. One of my books hit the ground.

"I'm really sorry," Jack said, leaning to pick it up, but I slammed the door and jammed in the key. All I wanted was to leave. Fast. I didn't know what I was doing on Hammond Island. I didn't belong here, and I certainly wasn't hanging around to be humiliated further.

"Anna," I barely heard Jack's voice as I punched the accelerator and drove away.

* * *

Thoughts swirled in my head as I drove across the narrow strip of land that separated the multi-million dollar estates from the rest of East End Beach. Jack's dad was exactly what I had expected — rich, powerful, and mean. *Difficult*, Jack had said. Right after he'd asked me out. And then took it back.

Right before his dad asked me about birth control. My face flashed hot.

This was stupid. All of it. I was not Cinderella, I had a plan. I was going to college and becoming a journalist. I was strong and this year was going to be different — and not the kind of different that included me being embarrassed by drunken businessmen. With incredibly sexy sons. Who lived in what was practically a palace on the beach. My heart sank as my thoughts drifted out the window and back to Jack Kyser. Incredibly sexy sons, who would be absolutely amazing to kiss...

I rolled down the window and breathed in the warm, salty air. It was a beautiful night, and soon my hands stopped shaking. The sun was a dim glow on the horizon, and the air was less hot in its absence. The black waves were crashing away. Seagulls and pelicans had roosted, and I could see the far-off lights of the city.

Twenty years ago, this place had been primarily farm families and society's drop-outs. But I knew from local talk that Bill Kyser was the hero of that story. His vision and ability to draw businesses to the area had transformed the place. Now it was awash in shiny green-glass high rises that made it look more like the Emerald City than a once-tiny farming village on the northeastern shores of the Gulf of Mexico.

I guessed that made him the wizard, and I liked the analogy better. He lived far away from the regular people who rarely saw him, if ever. He was very powerful and rich. And mean. I realized I didn't know much else about him other than his name, and that his wife died a long time ago.

Why would he isolate himself like that? He was from here, so he had to know a lot of people. And they might be small-town people, but the locals were all pleasant and friendly enough. Why would he withdraw? Was it grief after his wife died? Or was there something else?

My brow creased as I thought about my portfolio. Notable people. I wondered if my feature story could take a different approach. If I'd have the nerve to pursue it.

Chapter 4

The tardy bell sounded as I ran through the door and slid into my seat in English class. I didn't look to either side, but I could feel his eyes on me, and it made my stomach clench.

"That sound means you're *late*, Miss Sanders." Our teacher fixed her dark eyes on me. I gave her a pleading face, and to my surprise she softened. "I'll let this be your only warning."

"Thank you," I whispered, focusing on my book as she started the discussion.

She lectured right up to the bell, and as everyone was packing to leave, I saw Julian making his way through the bodies toward me. Sexy as ever, in black jeans with his shirttail out and sleeves rolled, everything about him should provoke a reaction in me, but something different was going on today. I was still thinking about the strange curtain I'd peeked behind last night, and despite it all, I wanted to know more. I wanted to be invited back.

"My patron saint of the arts," Julian smiled, sitting on my desk. "I've been looking for you all day."

"You're out of luck, Julian, I'm broke. Try Rachel or Brad."

"You can help me in more ways than money." He grinned, taking my hand.

I straightened. "What do you mean?"

"Go to the dance with me Friday. I'm dateless, and how would that look for your news story? It'd kill my image."

"It wouldn't kill anything but your pride," I slid my hand out of his. "And I don't know about Friday."

My voice trailed off as I glanced to the left, catching Jack's eye. He quickly turned back to digging in his backpack.

"You have to go with me," Julian insisted, standing. "You're my angel."

"Julian." I wanted to cut off his flirty rant. Jack would not understand it was just our usual banter.

But Julian moved in close, closer than he ever had. "Wear something sexy. I'll pick you up at seven." And out of nowhere, he leaned forward and kissed me.

Everything stopped. Julian's lips were touching mine. It wasn't a long kiss or French, but it was warm and soft. And it scrambled my brain.

"Julian!" I whispered, stunned.

His eyebrows went up and down, and his grin was classic Julian show-stopper. "You like? That was a little teaser."

I was still trying to remember what I'd been thinking when I saw my civics book on my desk. Jack was gone, and the next class was arriving. I was going to be late, and it appeared my fairytale dreams with him were over. But of course they were. He'd flat out said we shouldn't start anything, and his dad didn't like me.

"So we're on?" Julian said, backing up.

I blinked back to him. "Sure."

"Awesome." He smiled and disappeared as fast as he'd arrived, leaving me to sort out what just happened, and whether I was sad or thrilled.

Julian was far from sloppy seconds. I should be thrilled, but my brow lined. What was up with Julian? Was this about the feature? Could it honestly be more?

Could I honestly find out without looking like a total idiot?

* * *

Lucy didn't seem to know anything about what had happened at her house last night, which further reinforced my suspicion that my five-second flirt with dating her super-hot brother was over. But she did know about last period.

"So you're going to the dance with Julian LaSalle?" She eyed me curiously.

"Yeah. I'm doing a feature on his art for the newsblog. It's just research." I hadn't thought about the ethics of dating my subjects. Much.

"Sounds like a fun field," she winked. "Didn't he make the dolphin in the quad?"

I nodded. Last year Julian had designed a patchwork dolphin made up of discarded pieces of driftwood, copper, and metal roofing, and it turned out so well, the principal had it planted on the school grounds.

"He's really talented," I said. "His current project is a sculpture of a runner made from different pieces of junk. Like the head is a motorcycle tire and the arms and legs are metal tubing and stuff. It sounds weird, but it looks cool. He sent me some pictures."

She took my phone and slid her finger across the slideshow of Julian's art. "He does all this at school?"

"And his house. His mom basically gave him their garage for his workshop."

We were quiet as Mrs. Womack passed down the row returning graded projects.

"Are you going Friday?" I hoped she might tell me Jack's plans.

"Not sure," she whispered. "I don't really know a lot of guys here yet."

"Oh, well, it's just a silly dance." I didn't want her to feel bad—most guys at our school were probably too intimidated to ask Lucy on a date. And after meeting her dad, I wasn't sure they were wrong to feel that way. "I doubt I'd be going if Julian hadn't asked me."

"We got an *A* on our project." She smiled and turned back to her books.

Chapter 5

Even if I wasn't sure how to interpret my date with Julian, there would be pictures. And I wanted to look as hot as possible. Tamara Johnson had done my hair since we moved here, and being a local, she knew all the inside scoop. I sat in her home-salon Friday afternoon as she pulled out my curls with her big round brush and gave me the latest.

"Julian's so cute. I love the way he dresses. And so talented." She winked as if she knew something I didn't, which she probably did. "You know that running sculpture he's working on? With the motorcycle parts? His mom said it's been commissioned for the National Athletic Center in Darplane."

"That would be huge!" I had to add that to my feature on him—bonus for both of us! "Hey, I didn't know you did Ms. LaSalle's hair."

Julian got his easy, beachy manner straight from his mom. She reminded me of a French movie actress with olive skin, long dark-brown hair and dark eyes. She'd never married, not even Julian's dad, and she was quiet and graceful. I'd talked to her a few times when I was tutoring Julian. She owned a small souvenir and original artwork store down by the water.

"Oh, yeah," Tamara said. "Since we were kids. Before she was Alexandra LaSalle and just went by Lexy."

A one-word name. Perfect. "I wonder why she's always alone. She's so beautiful."

"Mm-hm," Tamara nodded. "Keeps to herself. Very private."

My mind drifted to the other loner I'd recently met. And my story idea. "Hey, what do you know about Bill Kyser? He has those twins who started at the school this year?"

"I know those folks don't mingle with the natives."

"Actually, Lucy invited me over to their house to study, and I sort of met him."

Tamara grinned. "Well, I will tell you this, *that's* a good-looking man."

"But kinda mean, don't you think?"

"I wouldn't know, baby girl."

"Do you know what happened to his wife?"

"Meg Kyser?" Tamara looked up at the ceiling. "It's been a long time. The official report is that she was killed in a car accident. Period. But there was some gossip drugs or alcohol was involved. I think some people even suggested she might've committed suicide. But that kind of stuff isn't said about the Kysers."

"Why would she do that?" I asked. "I mean, they're rich and she was a mom."

Maybe I could understand wanting to get away from Bill Kyser if he were as mean behind the scenes as out front, but I couldn't believe Jack and Lucy's mom would kill herself. She had small children, after all.

"Why does anybody do anything?" Tamara looked at me, and I knew what was coming. "Mental illness."

Tamara's big thing was mental illness ever since she'd started taking psychology courses at the community college. It was her explanation for everything these days.

"You think she was crazy."

"We don't like to use that term," she said. "But she might've had a hormone imbalance after having the twins, or maybe she was having an affair and got busted."

"Tamara!"

"Oh, I don't know anything for sure." Her dark eyes were twinkling as she laughed and finished ironing my last lock of hair. She spun me around so I was facing the mirror. "How's that?"

"Can we keep it this way forever?" I ran my hand down the side of my smooth, freshly highlighted coif. Tamara was very good at her job, and she didn't charge me full price since I was a minor, she said.

"Sorry, babe, those curls are coming back next wash. But hang in there. The fashion pendulum always swings back."

"Bye, Tam."

* * *

Once home, I ran straight to my room and pulled on my sundress from last spring. It still worked for fall being midnight blue with thin straps and flaring out nicely from my waist to my knees. I touched up my face, applied some red lipstick, and slipped on tan pumps, jogging back down the stairs just as Julian was walking in the door.

He looked great in jeans and a navy oxford that made his eyes glow. His dark hair was shiny and smooth with one lock hanging just past his eyes, and I watched him give my mom a quick hug.

"Y'all don't stay out late," she said. "We're headed to Navarre tomorrow, and I want to get on the road before noon."

"You got it. Back by dawn," Julian said, teasing her.

Then he saw me coming down and his eyebrows rose. I couldn't suppress a smile. "Nice," he said.

"Oh, stop." I answered, trying not to blush. "Let's go."

I took his arm as we walked out to his classic, light-blue Thunderbird. It was a convertible, of course, but he had the top up tonight. I mentally thanked the hair gods.

"I love your car," I said. "Very *Thunder Road*. Did you build it?"

"With Blake and Scotty," he held my door. "You ready to have some fun, fun, fun?"

"You bet. So, I take it welding is good for more than just making art?"

"Having friends in auto mechanics is also good." He closed my door and ran around to get in and start the engine. We rode for a few seconds listening to the radio. I looked out the window and couldn't help wondering if Jack would be at the dance.

"Hey, I heard your runner is headed to the National Athletic Center," I said. "That true?"

"Yep," he smiled at me. "And with your feature, my portfolio will be golden."

I shook my head. "I don't know if I'm important enough to help much. But once they see what you're doing in welding class, Savannah will be begging for you."

"Thanks." Julian gave me a meaningful smile, and conflict twisted in my middle.

I had the most idiotic luck of all time. The absolute most unexpected thing was happening—Julian LaSalle might actually want something more from me. And all I could think about was the other person I was hoping to see tonight. Why did this happen to me?

We made our way through the gym, and I waved to Rachel and Brad. The DJ played a slow song, and Julian led me onto the floor then pulled me close.

"I've been wanting to put the squeeze on you all night," he said, leaning his face to mine. We were practically nose to nose, with our bodies pressed together.

His hands massaged my waist, and my stomach tightened again. A full-on make-out session with Julian would be my ultimate, impossible dream-come-true. And here I was, standing on the edge of it, holding out that stupid hope for Jack. Pointless hope.

I tried to rationalize. On the other hand, my friendship with Julian was fun and cool, and what if this was just a one-night thing for him? He'd never been tied to any girl for more than a few dates—not even Renee. They were never a couple. So if he was just messing around, and I took him up on it, where would that leave our friendship?

It was one of those dilemmas that made fun television shows and sucky real-life problems.

"Julian," I said, putting a more friendly space between us. "Come on."

"You've been thinking about the same thing," he grinned. "Admit it."

"I've been thinking about algebra. How's that going?"

He chuckled at my deflection. "Like déjà vu. Very boring déjà vu."

"You're too smart to flunk a class, you know. Wasn't your mom ticked?"

"Mom doesn't hassle me about school."

"She doesn't hassle you about anything."

"Mom's cool, now back to us. When are we going out again? I was thinking…"

Just then I looked over Julian's shoulder and saw Renee Barron dancing with Jack. Of all people! Frustration duked it out with disappointment and confusion in my brain. Was that why Julian was suddenly so interested in me? Because Renee had taken up with Jack? And why was she here with Jack anyway? My lips twisted in a frown as I studied her smooth arms around his neck. Then she smiled and did a little hip movement. She knew how to work it. The corners of Jack's mouth rose and the last of my little hopes crashed and burned.

"Are you even listening?" Julian said.

I snapped back to him. "I'm sorry. What did you say?"

The song ended and everyone started to leave the floor. "Forget it. I'll get us a drink. Want something?"

"Sure."

Julian kissed my hand before he turned to walk over to the refreshments table. Dejected, I walked to the back of the gym, then outside to the small courtyard where the pep rallies usually occurred.

I did not expect to find Jack sitting on one of the tabletops. Immediately, my heart beat faster, my palms felt damp.

"Hey, Anna," he said.

"Hey." I glanced around. We were alone. "I just saw you dancing with Renee."

"Yeah. Lucy knows her. She wanted to come, so we doubled."

"Who's Lucy here with?" I hadn't even seen her.

"Steve Preston."

"Wow." I imagined Steve floating around in a dream as Lucy's date. It was how I'd feel with Jack. "That's cool. For him."

"And I saw you with Julian LaSalle," Jack fixed those blue eyes on me, and my head grew light. "I thought you said your boyfriend wasn't in shop class."

"He's not my boyfriend," I managed to answer. "I'm just doing a feature on him for the newsblog."

"Your subject seems very interested," he said. Was it possible he cared if Julian was interested in me? "Hey, about my dad—"

But a loud voice cut him off. "Jackie, my boy!"

Brad and Rachel strolled out and the guys clasped hands. "I talked to Coach, and he's onboard with letting you join the team," Brad continued. "So what's the holdup?"

"I don't know." Jack shifted, suddenly uncomfortable. "I don't really have time for sports."

"It's one semester!" Brad argued loudly. "I need a good wide receiver and with the way you run, you're it."

Rachel took my arm and gently pulled me aside.

"I like your hair," she said with a smile. "So you and Julian…?"

"Thanks, and no. I mean, we're just friends. But I think we'll get to say we graduated with a superstar before it's all over."

"And what about Jack?" She smiled in that knowing way. "I saw you talking to him just now. Looks like it's your night, girl."

"Is it?" I studied her face. She was Miss Guy-wisdom, after all, being the future Mrs. Brad Brennan. Eye-roll suppressed. "But I don't understand why. What happened?"

Rachel shrugged. "You're not hiding behind Gabi anymore. You're curious and open. And you've always been pretty. Guys like that."

I shook my head, but we were away from the group now. She pulled me close, my confusion back-burnered in favor of her scoop. "Get this—you are going to die."

I looked back and caught the reflection of light off a flask Brad was slipping from his breast pocket. He handed it to Jack, and I lost interest in whatever she was about to say. Getting suspended was not going on my permanent record.

"I'd better get back inside," I said.

"Forget about that. Nobody's going to bother Brad. Listen to what I found out." She leaned closer, lowering her voice. "Lucy got pregnant!"

"What?"

"That's what my mom said. That's why they're so old to still be in high school. Mr. Kyser shipped them off to their grandmother's in like Tacoma or someplace last year. Well, he shipped *her* off, and Jack went with her. Moral support or something."

"What are you talking about?" My head was spinning.

"The twins!" she cried. "They're turning nineteen next month. Didn't you get the invite to their party?" I had not. "So Lucy had an affair with her teacher, got pregnant, got expelled. I'm sure he was fired. Could've gone to jail if their dad had gone after him. Instead he shipped her into seclusion. Very hush-hush."

Apparently not hush-hush enough. I shook my swirling head. "No way. People don't do things like that anymore."

"Welcome to the Deep South." Her eyebrows went up knowingly as she nodded.

I had to say, if anyone would have the story, it would be Rachel's mom. And I hated to think of Lucy going through something like that. But why would Jack be sent away, too?

"Who cares?" I said. "Sometimes high school girls get pregnant. Big deal."

I started back to the gym, but just as quickly, Jack caught up to me. I stopped when his hand gently caught my arm. "Hey, wait a sec," he said.

Warmth flooded my body, starting at our point of contact. "Hey," I said softly, remembering my dream.

"You headed back inside?"

"Yeah," I said. "I-I can't get in trouble here."

"I'm sorry." He released my arm. "It's just Brad is so insistent."

I still wasn't sure how to take Rachel's story, and I hated that now I understood why he didn't want us to get involved. But it was hard to care about any of that when he touched me. "It's okay," I said. "You don't have to leave. I was just going back in—"

"Are you really not dating Julian?"

And there went all my logic. I studied his beautiful face and measured how much of a mistake it would be to say no. I knew in the center of my being this was my last chance to walk away and be okay with it. That if I took his hand, and he ultimately walked away, I'd never get over it. If only he wasn't so sexy...

Just then Julian appeared in the doorway. "Who moved the party?" He laughed, entering the courtyard and clasping hands with Brad, who slipped him the flask.

"Now how will I get home?" I said.

"Let me take you." Jack was holding my wrist again, and I was gone.

45

"I don't know if I want you driving me either," I said. "You've been drinking, too."

"Just a few sips. I'm fine, I promise." His blue eyes held mine. "Please? You'd be helping me out here."

"Helping you?" That didn't make sense. "But... What about Renee?"

"I'll see if she can catch a ride with Lucy and Steve. Look, it's the only way to get Brad off my back about damn football," he smiled, and I melted even more. I was doomed.

"I don't know," I started, but I knew I was going with him. "Julian might get his feelings hurt, and I don't want Renee mad at me."

"Let me handle it." He was off talking to Julian in an instant, and I was just standing there watching him. I couldn't take my eyes off him. My heart was flying in my chest, and I knew I wasn't in control of this anymore.

Rachel walked over smiling sideways at me. "You okay, Anna? You look dazed."

I shook my head and looked down, embarrassed. Julian made some mock-protest about me breaking his heart, holding his chest, then he walked over to join us.

"You're leaving me, Sunshine?" The smallest hint of disappointment in his voice killed me. Stupid, shitty timing.

"Not if you don't want me to." I hated that I only half-meant my words.

He studied my face for a moment, and my chest hurt at the expression in his eyes. *Julian*...

"It's okay," he said, his usual, easy laugh back. "If you want to go with him, I won't stop you."

Jack returned to the courtyard, and my eyes went from him to my date. "Do you want me to stay?"

Julian pressed his lips together. Then he leaned forward and kissed my head. "Don't do anything I wouldn't."

He waved me on, and I hesitated, almost deciding to stay until I saw Renee watching the whole thing, her eyes following Julian as he left me. I was sure she'd happily take care of him, and I told myself it was better that way. Then I took Jack's hand.

"See you Monday," he said to the group, and we walked to the lot where his Jeep was parked.

"Want to take the top off?" he asked.

"Um, no. My hair." I silently wished we lived someplace where the weather didn't turn my hair into cotton candy.

"I like it that way." He reached up and slid a piece off my neck. I felt a tingle as his hand gently grazed my shoulder. "But I like it the other way, too."

"What? A complete mess?"

"I've never seen it a mess."

"Have you ever looked at me?" My nose wrinkled.

"I don't think I've stopped looking at you for three weeks." My stomach did a double-flip. The thought of him checking me out was too much.

I cleared my throat, picking at my skirt and trying to recover. "Where are we going?"

"I was thinking we could head down to the beach?"

"The beach?" I knew where that would lead, and I was trying not to get emotionally involved too fast. Yeah, right. "O-okay."

He smiled and turned the wheel toward the Gulf Road, and in less than ten minutes we were running across the still-warm sand toward the water. Our shoes were left at the wooden boardwalk lining the state park.

We both stopped at the water's edge, staring out at the black horizon, and he caught my hand. I was breathing hard from the run and the anticipation, and for a moment, all I could do was stand there, looking into the distance, contemplating the future.

He turned and gently pulled me a half-step, and I was in his arms. A glint of blue, and his mouth covered mine. My lips parted, and the faintest taste of whiskey touched my tongue. I trembled as his hands traveled up the sides of my dress to my shoulders, then lightly cupped my cheeks. His lips moved to the corner of my mouth, then my jaw, and a tiny noise slipped from my throat. I was tense and electric, and all I could think were his soft lips touching me, my fingers exploring his hard stomach through the thin cotton shirt he wore.

His mouth traveled to my ear, where he kissed me lightly before whispering. "Let's sit."

Taking my hand, he sat in the sand and pulled me onto his lap. I watched as he unbuttoned his shirt, revealing his lined chest. Then he took my hands and placed my palms flat on his warm skin. Gorgeous.

"Now you," he said.

His arms circled to my back. I was breathing fast as he slid my zipper down, and my straps fell to the sides. I was sitting in my bra facing him in the silver moonlight, my hands still on his chest. My head was so light, I could barely breathe. This was all new to me, and there was no way I was stopping it. My shoulders shook, and I looked down.

"Are you afraid?" he whispered.

I shook my head no, lying. He cupped my chin, tilting my face up, and looked into my eyes. The breeze blew his golden hair around his cheeks, and I was convinced this was what an angel looked like.

"How old are you?" he said.

I bit my lip, not wanting to tell him I was only seventeen. Instead, I closed my eyes and leaned into his mouth again. Our lips parted, and his tongue found mine, circling as his fingers traveled across my skin, leaving goose bumps in their wake. They moved around to the front, tracing fiery lines along the edges of my bra. I shivered, and he stopped and pulled back, blue eyes meeting mine once more.

"I should take you home," he said, studying my face.

I was trying hard to keep it together and failing badly. All I could think of was his warm skin against mine and how much I wanted to press our bodies together.

"Really?" I said, wishing my voice didn't sound so timid.

"Yeah," he breathed, sliding the straps of my dress back to my shoulders and my zipper back in place.

I swallowed the lump in my throat. "I guess my mom is expecting me early. We're headed to my nana's tomorrow." Then I cringed. God, I was such a baby talking about my nana while making out at the beach with the hottest nineteen year old I'd ever seen in my entire life.

"Where?" he asked.

"Navarre. On the panhandle."

He nodded. "I know where it is."

My body was so buzzy and light as we walked back to the Jeep, I was sure I was levitating. Then we were inside and speeding back toward my house.

"I liked talking to you the other night," he said. "Maybe we could do that again sometime."

Talk? Was that was all he wanted now? Did my nervous stupidness somehow ruin my chance? Could I try again?

"I don't know," I said, trying to think of a way to seem more adult.

He glanced at me, hair blowing around his face. "I'm sorry I hijacked your night. I hope I didn't spoil your plans."

"No way. You didn't." Then I caught myself. *Be cool.* "I mean, it was unexpected. But not spoiled."

"And you definitely don't want to go out with me."

"What?"

"Lucy said you were very firm about it."

"Oh my god, she totally misunderstood." My hands went to my forehead. "I just didn't want her telling you that I told her to ask you to ask me out." *What did I just say?* "I mean, I didn't want you to get the idea that I was over here talking about you nonstop or something."

"So you never talk about me?" He started to smile again.

I paused, not knowing the right thing to say. Just because I didn't talk about him didn't mean I hadn't been thinking about him constantly.

"I don't really have anyone to talk to about you," I said.

"So you would talk about me if you had someone to talk to. About me." He was making fun of my confused statements, and I smiled then.

"I guess."

"You'll go out with me then?" His voice softened.

"You already asked me that," I said.

"But you never answered."

"I didn't?" I frowned, trying to remember.

50

"Okay, you did, but I didn't understand your answer. What did you mean you didn't know?"

"Honestly? I don't understand why you want to go out with me." I looked at my hands clasped in my lap, wondering why I had to ruin everything.

"Why wouldn't I?" He laughed.

"I'm not like you."

"Right. You're a girl. I like girls."

"No, I mean. You're from a different world, a different set of people. And I don't know a lot about that kind of stuff."

"I have no idea what stuff you mean."

"I mean, like going to fancy parties and talking about development and business." I didn't even go into my obvious lack of sexual experience.

"Hey," his tone changed. "About my dad, I'm really sorry. He drinks too much, and he was way out of line."

"Don't apologize. I'm sure it's a legitimate question these days with the way things are and all." I thought about the story Rachel had told me about Lucy.

"He was rude, and he embarrassed me," Jack said flatly.

"Yeah. I was a little embarrassed, too."

"So will you forgive my rude family and go out with me again?" We were in my driveway, and he came around to help me out.

"Your sister's not rude."

"What do you say?" Jack stopped me as I landed in front of him. I couldn't believe this was happening. I looked up and his blue eyes were right there, waiting for my answer.

"Okay. I mean, of course! Why wouldn't I?"

"Awesome." He smiled and kissed me lightly on the mouth. My heart stopped.

"I'll come by tomorrow," he said, walking me to the door.

"But I'm going to be at my grandmother's in Navarre." Yes, that sounded far more mature.

"Okay. I'll bring the boat down. I can put out in the Bay and meet you in the Sound."

Oh my god. And oh my god, his boat. Could I count on Mom and Nana to be cool?

"I don't know. I mean, my mom will be there and my grandmother…"

"I bet they're nicer than my dad."

Couldn't argue with that.

"Call you tomorrow," he said.

I nodded, studying his gorgeous face. Images of us kissing on the beach filled my head, and my whole body grew warm. I wished he would kiss me again, slower like before. But he was back in the Jeep and driving away before I'd had a chance to ask him how he knew where I lived.

Chapter 6

The next morning I was pushing Mom out the door.

"What time did you come in last night?" she complained. "I didn't hear you."

"Not late," I said still packing. "I didn't even look at the clock."

It was true. I'd floated in the house on a cloud and washed my face with stars and rainbows hovering around my head.

"I love Julian." Mom's eyes were still closed over her coffee. "I might steal him for myself."

"Yeah, about that." I stopped moving then. "I don't think I'm going out with Julian again."

"But he's so cute and funny!" My mom was whining. "And he's an artist. Artists are *so* romantic."

"Earth to Mom? Remember that fella who hangs around the house? We call him 'Dad'?"

"For you, baby. There's no reason why *you* can't be with someone romantic."

"It's not that," I said choosing my words. "Julian's great and all, but... well... there's somebody else I'm thinking about, and I'm kind of hoping that things work out with him instead."

"Who?" Mom was slowly waking up and her eyebrows pulled together.

"Umm... I don't think you know him."

"Name, please."

"John, or Jack Kyser?"

"Kyser." Mom frowned. "Is he related to the Kysers who own East End Beach?"

53

"They don't *own* East End Beach. His dad just developed a lot of the land down there. And yes. That's his dad."

Mom's eyebrows went up. "How in the world did you meet him? I heard those guys live out on Hammond Island and never... mix."

"He's in my English class at school."

"What?" she cried. "People don't know what they're talking about around here. I've been wanting to get Bill Kyser to donate to the performing arts association for years, and they're all, 'Jenni, don't waste your time—'"

"So, Mom," I interrupted her. "He's coming over to Nana's today. Is that OK?"

"Who? Bill?"

"MOM! Jack."

"Oh, of course! That'd be great. I'd like to meet him, but what? He's driving over?"

"I think he's bringing his boat." I cringed, waiting for her response.

"His boat?"

"I don't know." I tried to downplay it. "He said something about putting in at Lost Bay or something and bringing it up the Sound."

"He's got a boat?" Mom's grin made me squirmy. "Well, well."

"Mom. Please don't."

"Okay," she winked and took her cup to the sink. "But be careful. I don't want him taking you out to sea or anything like that. I heard there are pirates out there."

"Pirates? Seriously." I had to laugh.

"I'm just telling you what I heard."

"Well, don't worry," I said. "I don't think we're headed out to sea anytime soon."

* * *

Navarre Beach was possibly one of the most beautiful places on Earth, and Nana's condo was right on the water. The white sand was grainy and covered in shells, and the glassy water turned from turquoise to deep marine blue as it stretched toward the horizon. The beachfront community was very small, and only a narrow strip of land separated the Gulf from Santa Rosa Sound. When we got there, Nana was out walking on the shore, picking up shells and tossing them into the water.

"Nana!"

I loved visiting her. Even though she was in her mid-70s, she was still as sharp as ever. "Anna," she smiled. "You look like you're adjusting to school well, and I like the straight hair."

"It won't last long out here, but thanks. School's great. I miss Gabi, but I've met some new people. It's not as bad as I expected."

"And boys? Who's dating my sweet granddaughter now?"

"Well, I don't know about the 'now' part, but there is a potential love interest on my horizon."

"He doesn't deserve you." She winked.

"Maybe. We're still working out the details."

Nana laughed, and we walked up to the house to see Mom. Dad stayed back in Fairview so it would be just the three of us tonight. After Jack left, of course.

Even though Nana had a beach-front condo, we weren't rich. She'd combined the sale of her old house, Pop-pop's life insurance and some of their retirement to buy the place almost a decade ago, and so far, she'd been able to weather any storms that came along. Nana said she'd rather scrape by on a meager income and be on the beach than be rich and landlocked. I tended to agree with her after seeing her beach.

"I'm going to walk over and set up on the Sound side today." I picked up my straw tote and beach gear.

"What's that? The Sound side?" Nana knew I preferred being near the Gulf.

"A boy's bringing his boat up from Hammond Island to meet her," Mom explained.

"His boat? I approve!" Nana sounded like Mom. "And I'd like to meet this boy with the boat."

"I'll see if that can be arranged." I winked and ran out the door. I hadn't gone far when my phone buzzed. It was Jack.

"Ay, ay, captain! Where are you?" I was excited and nervous at the same time.

"The bay. I should be there within the hour."

"Call me when you're closer."

I couldn't wait, so I got up and started walking west down the Sound. Before long, I saw a sail in the distance and grabbed my phone, punching up his number.

"Jack here."

"Hey, is that you I see?"

"What? Anna? Where are you?"

"I'm walking on the beach," I said as I waved my arm. "How can I get to you?"

"Hang on, let me see what I can do."

It wasn't long before I saw him loosening the sails and maneuvering the boat to a crawl. It was a beautiful craft, not terribly large, but breathtaking with shimmering brown wood and shining brass rigging. He must've dropped the anchor, because next thing I saw, he was stripping off his shirt and diving into the water. A few minutes later, we were sitting on the sand together, him dripping wet and half dressed. Today was going even better than I'd expected.

"Well, aren't you something," I giggled.

"Sailing is… well, it's the greatest thing in the world."

"It does look wonderful," I smiled. "Does it take long to learn? I've never been on a sailboat."

"I could teach you the basics in an afternoon, and then it's just practice, learning to keep out of trouble." He glanced at me. "You want to swim out? I can help you onboard."

I paused at that suggestion. "I heard there are sharks in the Sound. Big ones."

"They won't bother us," he said, getting up and reaching for my hands.

"So not encouraging!" I laughed. "But I don't have anywhere to put my cover-up. And this…" I held out my phone.

"I think I can hold them up while I swim. Come on," he said, taking my stuff.

I followed him cautiously toward the water. "Is it true I should just punch the shark in the nose, and he'll leave me alone?" I tried to joke.

Jack shook his head. "Just swim to the boat. You'll be fine."

In a few strokes he was helping me up the short ladder onto the deck. I was soaked, and my straight hairstyle was ruined. But the boat was amazing. Even more amazing was watching Jack with his shirt off loosening the anchor and tightening the sails. His tanned muscles flexed, and I completely forgot about the beauty of our surroundings.

"You do this all the time?" I asked, pulling my wet swimsuit away from my stomach and wishing for my cover-up. Even though I'd spent the summer in a bikini, I wore a one-piece today. I wasn't quite ready to bare that much skin with him in broad daylight. He didn't seem to mind.

"As much as I can," he smiled, sitting beside me. "I really missed it when we were in Sedona last year."

"What's in Sedona?"

"My mom's mom, Gigi. Lucy and I were out there last spring all the way up until school started back."

"Why?" I was wondering if Rachel's story had been true.

"Oh, family stuff. I don't think it's anything you'd find interesting." I wanted to tell him everything about him was very interesting to me, but I didn't. Because just then my phone buzzed.

"It's probably my mom."

I smiled as Jack handed it back to me, but he saw the face when I took it. "Julian," he said.

My eyes went wide. "What?" I said with a nervous little laugh. I could tell Jack didn't believe my shocked expression. "He never calls me."

"It's okay." He stood and went over to readjust the line. I let Julian's call go to voicemail. *Oh my god!*

"You guys are pretty close," he said.

"Just since last year. I mean, I tutored him in math."

"I saw you dancing. You looked — "

"Julian flirts with everybody," I cut him off. "Seriously. We're just friends."

He shrugged. "Okay."

Frantically I searched for anything else in the world to talk about. "My grandmother's dying to meet the boy with the boat."

"Would she like to come sailing with us?" His smile returned.

"I'm sure she'd love it. Mom, too."

"Then let's get them."

We tied up the boat in the marina and walked down the shore toward Nana's condo. "I'm glad you wanted to come over today." I said, hoping to remove any lingering doubt caused by Julian's call.

Jack smiled. "I like being with you, and Saturdays can be long at our house."

Hearing those words made *me* smile. He liked being with me. Then I remembered that first night and how he changed when his dad appeared.

Hesitantly, I asked, "You don't get along with your dad?"

He exhaled, "It's not that. He's never really around. I just get tired of the same people and doing the same things all the time. My friends don't have a lot of imagination."

"What would you do on a typical, unimaginative Saturday?"

"Sleep 'til noon…"

"Spoiled!" I pretended to be shocked.

He grinned. "Most likely I was out late the night before. But then I'd either go for a run or take the boat out."

"No girls? I don't believe it."

"I've taken a few girls out, but they get tired of sailing and want to go shopping or hit the spa or something like that. It's pretty boring after a while, I guess."

"I think it sounds great. I'd love to try getting bored with sailing."

"I can help you with that."

He seemed to mean it, and I was glad to spend the rest of the day taking Mom and Nana out with us. They were easy to spend time with, and they both seemed to like Jack very much by the end of the afternoon.

The sun was setting when he said it was time for him to go. I walked down the beach with him a little ways. "I had so much fun today," I said.

"Me, too. I liked your nana. And your mom."

We walked a little further, and I was wondering if he would bring up our unscheduled date again when he reached over and took my hand. Our fingers laced, and I forgot about everything else. We were holding hands, walking on the beach. In the sunset. The only thing better was the way he kissed me last night.

After a few seconds, he stopped and turned to face me. "You should probably stay here while I walk back to the marina." His voice was slightly lower, and I nodded. He leaned in a little closer. "I was wondering if I could kiss you goodnight."

It just got better.

"You have to ask?" I said with a smile.

"I felt like last night, maybe I went too fast?"

I stepped forward, gripping the front of his shirt and tilting my chin up. "I don't mind fast."

He smiled and leaned in, covering my mouth with his. Our lips parted, and when his tongue touched mine, heat flooded, heart-stopped, knees weakened... I wasn't sure how it could be better than last night, but somehow it was. He lifted his head, and I didn't dare speak. I was afraid I might blurt out something ridiculous like "Do it again."

"So I'll call you tomorrow?" he asked.

I nodded. He walked away, but before he got too far down the beach, he turned and did a little wave. I giggled and waved back, watching as he continued on.

Chapter 7

The smile did not leave my face the rest of the weekend. Everything happened in a colorful blur, and when my phone rang Sunday morning, it was Jack. I jumped up and snatched it and then tried to be cool.

"Hello?"

"I know I was supposed to make you sick of sailing, but Sunday's golf day." He said. "I'll be out at Laurel Farms all day with Dad."

Laurel Farms was one of the nicest golf courses in the county. Or so I'd heard. It was now my least favorite place on the planet.

"Golf day?" I said, my smile disappearing.

"Yeah, Dad likes me to work on my game. Something about all the best deals are made on the golf course."

"Is that true?"

"I don't know. He doesn't really like to talk when we're golfing. My take is the deals are made after the game. Over scotch and cigars at the clubhouse."

"Are you included in that part, too?

I heard his exhale. "Sometimes. Off the record, of course."

"Well, I hope you make it to class tomorrow. Essay's due, you know."

"I was thinking about that," he perked up. "How 'bout I pick you up on my way in?"

"You mean drive me to school?" Smile returning! Still being cool. "Sure, I'll see you tomorrow then."

I thought about riding to school with Jack Kyser and wondered how that would play out with our fellow classmates. Rachel would be all over me trying to get the inside story, and I was sure Julian would act disappointed. Then I remembered his call, but just as I grabbed my phone, Dad tapped on my door.

"Hey, kiddo. Mom said you had a visitor yesterday. Somebody with a yacht?"

The word *yacht* made me want to giggle more, and I was about to correct him. But I let it go. I was seeing a guy with a yacht. What had happened in a month?

"Yeah, remember the Kysers? I went over to their house to study that night?"

"I remember, and I wanted to talk to you about that." Dad wasn't smiling, and I was suddenly feeling less sure of my mom's approval of Jack. He walked over and sat on my bedside next to me. I could tell he was choosing his words. "Those guys are a bit, well, over your head."

"I know, Dad, but Jack's really nice. You'd like him."

"I'm sure, but I want you to take it easy with this guy. You're a pretty girl, Anna. You're smart and a good writer. Your mom and I think you could probably get a scholarship to a bigger college if you wanted to try for something like that."

"I hadn't really thought about trying for a scholarship." I hadn't thought about much of anything except Jack since school started.

"Just keep your eye on the prize, and don't let some guy control your future, okay?"

"That's a good way to look at it." My eyes flickered down as I considered my dad's approach versus Mr. Kyser's. He patted my leg and got up to leave. "Oh, hey, Dad? I meant to ask you. I kind of already said yes, but

Jack asked if he could pick me up for school in the morning. That's okay, isn't it?"

"I think that's a great idea. Give me a chance to meet this yacht-boy."

His sudden enthusiasm made me very concerned. This had disaster written all over it. "Please don't be embarrassing."

"I wouldn't dream of it."

"And no bananas. Please."

"But you're my Anna-banana. He needs to be aware of this."

"Dad."

"Okay, no bananas. Just remember what I said."

"Sure." I picked up my phone again when I saw I had a message. "Julian," I murmured, pressing the voicemail button.

His voice was casual as always. "Hey, banana-face, what's up with the voicemail?" I rolled my eyes as I listened. He'd almost ruined everything. "Just making sure you got home okay. I'm sorry we got separated." He paused then cleared his throat. "So anyway, see you around."

I stared at the phone for a second then touched the face, saving the message. I went to my laptop and opened a new document. I could at least get his news feature written before any more time passed.

Chapter 8

Jack was very punctual picking me up for school, and I was almost late after trying ten different uniform combinations hoping for the sexiest. Why my hair had to look the way it did was my own personal burden, but I noticed my clothes were a little looser. Having a hot potential-boyfriend kept my stomach so twisted, my appetite had virtually disappeared. My last snack-out had been my miserable night with *The Notebook.* It was simply impossible to be sad now with Jack in the picture, and I loved the racing butterflies. They made me feel all bubbly and amazing.

I finally settled on the navy skirt option with a light-blue polo and brown flats when I heard him downstairs talking to my dad. I jerked my hair back in a ponytail and ran down hoping to derail any discussion of me as a baby, or bananas, or other embarrassing topics.

"Hey!" I was breathless when I reached the kitchen, and Jack's smile when he saw me didn't help.

"You look nice," he said.

Dad cleared his throat, "So be careful on the roads."

"Sure, Dad. See you tonight."

When we drove into the parking lot, I noticed a few heads turn. "How'd Lucy get here?" I asked.

"She has her own car."

I noticed a bright yellow Cabrio parked in the next space and wondered what it would be like to grow up getting whatever you wanted. Jack helped me out, then he took my book bag and slid his arm across my shoulders. "Maybe we should do this every morning."

"That'd be great!" My voice sounded squeaky to me, so I cleared my throat. He was just so confident and rich and gorgeous. I imagined everyone as bewildered by this turn of events as me.

"How was golf?" I said.

"The same," he looked away, and I noticed his jaw tighten. "The course was hot. Dad talked nonstop about my future. But I shot a two under."

"And you lost me."

"I'd rather have been teaching you to sail."

"I can't wait. How soon can we start lessons?"

"Not this weekend," he frowned. "We're headed to New Orleans to visit my brother and let Lucy tour Tulane."

"Tulane? Your brother?" I stopped and faced him. "Fill me in."

"William's working on his MBA at Tulane, and Dad's talking about enrolling her there."

"William." I thought about what my dad said. "So, like, Bill, Jr.?"

"He's named after my dad, but he's not really called that."

"What? Junior or Bill?"

"Neither. But he does like to think they're exactly alike."

"He wants to be exactly like your dad?" We started walking again, and I considered Mr. Kyser's cold eyes and rude remarks.

"Yeah, but he doesn't really get Dad." Jack looked down still frowning. "Will's all power and conquest, and Dad's not really into that. He just likes a good deal. He's not ruthless."

"Is William ruthless?"

"He wants to take over, and he wants me right there with him."

"What do you think about that?"

"I think I'm happy where I am." He gave me a squeeze, and we were at English.

I looked up at his bright blue eyes and wondered if he was thinking the same thing as me—kissing on the beach, moonlight, skin against skin...

* * *

Lucy cornered me in civics right off acting annoyed. "You big faker. 'I do *not* want to date your brother. Please don't embarrass me.'" She used this high falsetto voice to mock me.

"Sorry. I guess I got swept off my feet."

She giggled, "I think it's great. I just want it on the record that it was my idea. I was ready to put you two together from Day One."

"I know—but why? I mean. I'm having trouble figuring this one out."

"Oh, you're just what he needs. Quiet, thoughtful, smart."

"Am I quiet and thoughtful?"

"Please." Lucy rolled her eyes at me.

"Hey, so you're going to Tulane this weekend?"

"Jesus. Don't remind me." Her expression changed completely. "Yay. We get to spend the whole weekend with my asshat older brother so Dad can decide if he should ship me to live with him." Then her eyes took on an expression much like her dad's. "So he can keep his eye on me nonstop. At least Jack will be there."

I thought about what Rachel had said about Lucy's past. I'd never expected to see that cold Bill-Kyser glare in her eyes. Of course, I hadn't known her that long. Then I thought of Jack saying their brother was ruthless.

More strangeness. More mystery. I wondered if I'd ever know what really happened to make their family this way.

* * *

Julian caught up to me that afternoon while I dragged my Calculus book out of my locker. "There you are," he said. "Heartbreaker."

"I got your message. You were just kidding with all that, right? You didn't care that I left—"

"That you ditched me for the clichéd alternative?" He leaned against the locker next to me, grinning. "No worries. Things turned around."

"I filed your story today with those pictures you sent me. It'll go to all the local news outlets. Prepare to be a superstar."

"That's my girl," he caught one of my curls and gave it a little tug.

I glanced and spotted new ink, a tiny dragonfly tattoo just above his right thumb. "Hey, let me see." I caught his hand and studied the detailed drawing. "What's the story of this little guy?"

"More logo hunting," he said, running his finger over it. "Like it?"

"You're getting really good at this." My eyes drifted to his blue ones, and I smiled. "Just like all your art. So what does it mean?"

"Change, deeper understanding, happiness." His fingers lightly curled around my hand. "It actually symbolizes different things in different cultures. In China it's good luck."

"I think it's my favorite." With a squeeze, I let him go.

His lips pressed together briefly. "So what do you think about Lucy Kyser?"

"I think she's gorgeous. And unexpectedly sweet."

"I think you're right, and after you left, she introduced herself. We talked about art and welding and—"

My eyebrows rose. "You hooked up with Lucy?"

"Sadly, there was no hook-up. But her skin is so soft, and she smells so good..."

"Julian. Please."

He laughed. "Okay. It was all very innocent, but I'm thinking of taking it up a notch. Have you heard about this birthday party they're having?"

UGH! Yes I'd heard, and no I hadn't been invited. Yet.

"Seems like Rachel said something about it." I pretended not to care.

"Well, I met this lady, this artist, in Newhope who makes jewelry. Helen Freed?"

I shook my head no, and he continued.

"I was thinking about trying her technique and maybe putting something together for Lucy. Like a gift." As always his blue eyes sparkled when he talked about his art. "It's smaller work, more delicate and using a soldering iron. But I figure I need to be versatile. So would you help me?"

"Julian!" I exhaled loudly, resting my head on my locker. "My mom was totally right about you."

"Your mom's hot. What did she say?"

"Just that artists are so romantic, and look at you. That is very romantic."

He frowned. "I was aiming for thoughtful. And 'expanding my range.'"

"Well, I think it's romantic, and Lucy will flip if you make her a piece of jewelry. I know I would."

"You would?" His tone changed slightly.

"Besides," I continued, "she has everything. What other kind of present could you give her?"

"And then you kick me in the nards. Thanks, Banana-face."

I pretended to frown. "I prefer Sunshine. And I'm just saying. I'm completely in the same boat over here."

"Yeah, so you're really going out with that guy? I expected more from you. It's disappointing."

I shrugged. "I don't know. We haven't DTR'd."

"Translation?"

"Defined the relationship."

"Well, the party's at their house, so if you need a ride, let me know. I don't really want to drive over there alone."

"That would be great!" I perked up at the thought. "I will."

* * *

Jack was waiting for me at the Jeep, ticking my heart up as always with his perfect face. Only this time the face didn't look happy.

"I saw you chatting with your friend Julian." He nodded in the direction from which I'd just come.

"Oh," I looked back, but Julian was gone. "No. I mean, nothing to fear there. It seems Lucy has worked her magic on him."

"Really?" His expression didn't change.

"Disapprove? I can vouch for him. Julian's a great guy."

"I'm not worried about her, but Lucy tends to be careless in relationships."

"She's a player?"

"Not really. More looking for a hero or something." He took my bag and placed it in the back seat.

"Well, Julian's very artistic. I don't know if that counts as heroic."

"And he's one of your shop guys. Aren't they all heroes in your book?" He was teasing me now, but I was glad he wasn't frowning. I started to climb in the Jeep, but his hand went to my waist.

"Hey, slow down," he said.

Then he leaned in and gave me a long, soft kiss on the lips. Everything around us faded away, and my fingers fumbled to hold his starched oxford. He lifted his head and smiled.

"Thanks." I said, breathless.

Then he laughed. "Thanks?"

I felt myself blush. "I don't know. That was nice? I wasn't expecting a kiss."

"C'mon. I've got to get you home."

* * *

The whole weekend I didn't get a single call or even a text from Jack. I tried not to be miserable, but I hated it. Nothing interested me, and I just wanted to hear his voice and stir up the butterflies again.

I tried to console myself. He was touring the college, and it was rude to be on the phone all the time when you visited someone, right? Finally, Sunday night, a text appeared saying I'd have to drive myself to school. I was a little concerned, but I figured I could wait a bit longer and see him in class. I wanted another kiss, but we had time for that.

Jack never made it to class, and Lucy wasn't in civics. I was worried when I bumped into Julian, and he told me Lucy had come back from New Orleans with a virus and was staying home. Still, why was Julian hearing from Lucy, but I wasn't hearing from Jack?

I tried to call him and got voicemail, so I left a message and waited. It was hard to concentrate on class work, but I made it through the day, back home, and through supper. He still hadn't called by bedtime, so I tried one more time to call him and got his voicemail again. This was getting weird. If Lucy had a virus, it was possible Jack could have it too... I wished I'd asked Julian if it was a stomach bug or just fever and went on to bed.

I slept poorly, and the next morning I waited until 7:40 to decide I must be taking myself to school again. I was almost tardy to Mrs. Bowman's class and dashed in just in time to see Jack's empty seat. Now I was really worried. After school, I tried his cell again, and when his voicemail answered, I decided not to leave a message this time. I decided to drive to his house.

* * *

The sun was setting, but it was still 80 degrees when I parked in front of the house on Peninsula Avenue and got out. Suddenly I felt silly and impulsive. What was I doing? We weren't officially dating yet. Did one mini make-out session, a drive to school, and a few follow-up kisses count as a relationship? I wasn't sure.

Now what? Did I barge in and demand to see him? His dad didn't even like me, and I knew Lucy was sick.

What if Jack were puking his guts up? I'm sure he really wanted me to see him like that. I was about to ditch the whole idea and drive home again when I heard the clink of ice on crystal.

"Hello?" A man's voice called. "Can I help you?"

The figure that emerged from the side patio this time was not Mr. Kyser. He was tall like Mr. Kyser and had the same light brown hair and cold blue eyes, but this guy was about twenty years younger.

"Oh!" I said. "You must be William!"

"I'm sorry," he smile-frowned. "It seems you know who I am, but I don't know you. Are you one of Lucy's friends? Do you live here on the island?"

"Um, yes and no," I was trying to be friendly, but it didn't seem to cut the tension. "Lucy and I have class together, but I live in Fairview."

His expression morphed to one of disapproval, and he seemed finished with me at once. "Lucy's not seeing anyone right now. She has a cold."

"I heard it was a virus. Is Jack sick, too?"

"What's your interest in Jack?" His voice was irritated, and my hands felt clammy. So much for being friends.

"I, uh. Well, he's in my English class, and he wasn't at school. I didn't know if he might be sick or need my notes or something."

"Are you Anna?"

"What?"

"You are. Dammit, Dad! This is worse than I thought." He wasn't talking to me, and I decided that was my cue to leave.

"I'm sorry, maybe I should go."

"Maybe you should, and don't come back." His voice was stern. Mean, even.

"Your little fling with my brother is over," he said.

My eyes blurred, and I was having trouble finding the handle of my car. This scene was all too familiar — me being humiliated at Jack's house. I barely heard the sound of footfalls coming up the road when I recognized his familiar voice.

"Anna? Hey! William?"

"Your friend was just leaving," William said.

"Shut up, Will. Anna? Are you OK? What are you doing here?" Jack was at my side, and he at least sounded concerned. He didn't look sick at all.

"You weren't at school, and I tried to call..." My voice trailed off. I was desperately trying not to cry. I wanted to throw my arms around him, but he was wet from running or swimming or both. Who knew?

He squeezed my arm. "Hang on, let me put on some dry clothes. You want to come inside?"

He seemed glad to see me, but William took a sip from his tumbler and glared at me.

"I'll wait here," I said. "Will you be long?"

"Two seconds. Please wait," he pleaded. "Will, come inside."

"Gladly." His brother sounded disgusted.

I stayed by my car while the two went into the house. The door didn't completely close, and I could hear part of their conversation.

"Don't talk to my friends." Jack's voice was sharp.

"What are you going to do?" William scoffed. "Fight me?"

"I'd love to. Let's go."

"Will you ever be more than my punk-assed little brother?" William sighed. "Dad made a stupid decision sending you to public school. Bryant Brennan might not care what his son does, but you certainly aren't getting mixed up with some girl who'll just get you in trouble."

I felt my face grow hot. *Not this again.*

"You don't know anything about Anna," Jack's voice sounded like he was pulling a shirt over his head.

"And you're thinking with your dick."

"You're the dick," Jack growled. "Don't talk to my friends."

"These are not your friends, and soon enough you'll be where you belong."

Jack returned looking incredibly handsome in a white t-shirt and loose khakis. I had missed him, and now I felt like I was about to lose him. My throat tightened.

"Hey, come on. Let's walk down to the Bay," he said.

"What's going on?" I said, trying not to sound desperate. "Why is he here? Why haven't you been at school?"

He took my hand and pulled it to his lips for a kiss. "I thought about you the whole time we were gone," he said smiling. "What did you do all weekend?"

"Who cares what I did! What's happening? What did William mean about being where you belong?"

"You heard that," he frowned.

"You didn't answer my texts, and I tried to call —"

"Come on." He put an arm across my shoulders, and we walked down Peninsula Avenue in silence. I was starting to get worried when we reached the shore of Lost Bay and he still hadn't said a word.

He sat down on the sand and gently pulled me down beside him and into his side. We listened to the gentle ripples of the water. It was more like a lake on this side of the island, but I couldn't relax. I looked up at the sky just getting dark.

Finally he spoke. "Lucy's got a big mouth."

"What happened this weekend?" I felt like I was going to die if he didn't tell me something.

"What I told you — going to New Orleans, meeting with Tulane officials, touring the campus. Then William started asking questions about what we were doing now. Lucy talks a lot when she's nervous, and he makes her very nervous." Jack laced our fingers together and stroked the inside of my forearm.

"But why would your brother care about me?" My voice sounded too desperate, but it was hard to hide my feelings. "Other than to note our differences, I mean."

"We're not so different," he smiled. "My family's just been here longer. Your dad's in development, right?"

"Sort of. He's a contractor."

"Well, suppose you guys had lived here fifteen years ago, and he'd been one of the men on the golf course. We could be neighbors."

"But would you notice the girl next door? You seem to prefer going outside the box."

"Would the girl next door have such cute curls or cry at the end of *Song of Solomon* or want to learn to sail with me?"

"Yes."

"Then you bet I'd notice her."

I pressed my cheek against his shoulder still worried. He smiled and gently lifted my chin and kissed me. It was a soft kiss, then a little nibble, a little touch of his tongue. As always, it lit me right up, but my chest was tight. It was hard to breathe. He pulled me around so I was facing him, my back toward his knees, and slid the band out of my hair, spreading out my curls.

"What are you doing?" I tried to fight him and pull them back into a knot.

"I love these." He grabbed one lock that had managed to hold together in a large spiral and pulled it around in front of my face.

"Well, too bad there aren't more of those. The rest are just fuzz," I tied my hair back again. "So you didn't tell me what William meant by 'where you belong'? Why is he here?"

"He's trying to convince Dad we should graduate mid-year. Start college in the spring."

My heart slammed to the ground, and I knew he could see the look on my face, even in this light.

"He won't do it?" I whispered.

"I don't know. William makes a good point that we're really just wasting time now. We've got the credits. There's no reason to wait."

"But what about Lucy? I'm sure she doesn't want to leave so soon."

"That's where you come in. She panicked. It seems your artist-friend made a real impression on her, and she flipped out at dinner going on about how she couldn't leave Julian. Said I wouldn't want to leave you. Threw us right under the bus."

"What did you say?" I asked quietly.

"I didn't say anything. Lucy's not smart enough to know the best way to handle those two is to tell them as little as possible. Of course, Will had to take a few days off to come home and see what's going on here."

"What's his problem?"

"He's worried about our future, meaning me. Says we should be moving into the Gulf market, making more investments in South America, the Caribbean. He's ready for me to get in the business now, and if he has to wait another year, he's worried there won't be any prime real estate left. It's already disappearing fast."

"Is that even safe? I mean, hurricanes regularly wipe everything out, and with global warming and all, won't it just happen again?"

"Listen to you," Jack chuckled. "What do you know about these things?"

"I hear my dad talking."

"That was a concern immediately after the last big storm, but now it's been several years and things are getting back to normal."

"So you'll start working with him in college?" I frowned, but it made sense. "I guess I can understand why your brother wants you with him."

"Will's just greedy. Dad's made enough good decisions to keep us comfortable for a long time. Leave something for the rest of the world. And get off my back," Jack's anger had returned.

"I take it he doesn't agree with you."

"He thinks I'm lazy." It sounded like he was repeating an old argument.

"You're not lazy. I mean, I guess you are coasting this semester, but you did the work once already. If it weren't for your concern for Lucy —"

"What do you know about that?" His sudden sharpness made me hesitate.

"Rachel said something about it being Lucy who got expelled, and you dropped out to save her reputation or something."

"Rachel doesn't know what she's talking about." Jack looked off.

"What did happen?" I asked softly. "I mean, it's personal. And maybe you don't know me well enough yet..."

He smiled that gorgeous smile and leaned forward to brush his lips over mine. His breath whispered across my cheek, and my heart skipped a beat. It was so nice when he did that.

"It's really Lucy's business," he said. "So I hope you can keep this to yourself."

"Of course! I mean, who would I tell?"

"Rachel?"

"Oh, god no. Rachel's a big mouth. I didn't even tell her about us. I mean, it was obvious when you started driving me to school and all, but she would've been the last person—"

"You would've talked to if you'd had someone to talk to about me?"

"Right." I smiled and slid my fingers under his bangs, smoothing them out of his eyes like I'd always wanted to do.

His voice turned serious as he told me the story. "Well, I told you Lucy likes to find a hero."

"Right. Although, I think you're her real hero."

"She got involved with an older man who took advantage of his position, and she ended up pregnant. He blamed her for the whole thing, said she'd entrapped him, and insisted she have an abortion."

My brow creased. "Oh, god. Poor Lucy."

"Dad pulled her out of school and sent her to Sedona, to Gigi, and found an adoptive family for the baby."

"But why did you go?"

"I got expelled."

"What?" He said it so casually, I thought I'd misunderstood. "Why?"

"I met the guy in the parking lot one afternoon and beat the shit out of him. Brad and a few of his football buddies helped me. Somebody called the cops, but they took a long time getting there. Played out nicely."

My mouth dropped open for a moment. Then I closed it. This was new, and I wasn't sure how to interpret it. "Were you... arrested?"

His lips tightened. "Dad's lawyer handled it. The bastard decided letting me off was better than getting charged with statutory rape."

I didn't answer immediately; more questions were answered. "I guess your dad was pretty angry."

"I think he was more pissed I might lose my chance at Yale." Jack looked off again and the tension was back. "I asked to go to Sedona. Lucy was a mess, and I figured some time with Gigi would be nice. She pretty much raised us."

"So Lucy never considered... the alternative?"

"What? Abortion? We're Catholic, Anna. And, well, I don't think she could've gone through with that."

"Oh, right. Of course not. I didn't mean she should've or anything. It's just she was so young, and you guys have so much money..." I wasn't sure how to finish that sentence, so I switched gears. "You're really sweet to her."

He seemed to relax. "She gets ignored a lot. She frustrates Dad, and William thinks she's clueless. But she just wants attention from somebody. It's been hard for her not having a mom around."

"Do you remember your mom?"

"Not really," he smiled. "I mean, we were three when she died. I remember her soft hair and smile, feeling good when I was with her. But that's about it."

His words made my chest hurt. "That's really sad."

"Yeah, well, it was a long time ago. We never talk about it."

That statement seemed odd, and I wondered how much of what Tamara said was true. But I decided not to pursue it. He'd told me so much already.

"Will you be at school tomorrow?" I asked.

"No. We're supposed to meet with the administrators to talk over scheduling. And Dad wants to make the case that my time in Sedona taught me anger management."

"You warned me your life was complicated," I sighed. "I guess I didn't believe you."

He looked down. "I'll understand if this is more than you bargained for. We can be friends or —"

"No! That's not what I want at all!" I threw my arms around his shoulders and hugged him close. "I really wanted to come here tonight. I was worried about you, and... I don't want you to leave."

My voice cracked, and tears filled my eyes. I knew the day he left this dream I was having would end, and I could hardly bear the thought.

He exhaled, and I pressed my forehead against his warm neck. Before long his hands moved to my sides, lightly massaging, and I lifted my face searching for his kiss. Our lips met, and when his tongue found mine, that delicious warmth filled my body. He moved me to lying back on the sand and leaned down, kissing me deeper. I slid my hands to his cheeks, trying to hold on as his mouth moved mine open again. My breath quickened, and his kisses traveled to my face and then to my neck.

His hand slipped under my shirt, tracing a burning trail up my stomach. My heart was skipping, but I wasn't stopping him. All I could think was this might be my last chance, our last time together.

My eyes fluttered open. The sun had almost completely set, and everything was bathed in a deep, orange glow. Jack moved away and in one swift pull, his shirt was over his head and off. My hands spread across his chest, golden and beautiful, with just a few fine hairs scattered across the top. He leaned in again to find my mouth, and I slid my hands down, exploring his warm torso. He groaned and pulled me up, straddling his lap. I could feel where this was headed as he fumbled with the hem of my loose cotton skirt, making his way beneath it to my panties.

Heat was surging through me, and I wanted to follow him. I did. My hands moved to his wrists, hesitantly holding them as his fingers found what they were seeking. But when he touched me, I made a little noise and slid off his lap.

"Hang on," I gasped, releasing him and then holding my cheeks as my heart tried to settle. "This is just so... well... It's awfully public."

Jack lay back on the sand and pressed his palms against his eyes. I could see he was breathing fast, and for a moment, we didn't speak. I looked down. The tiny ripples of water continued to break on the shore, and I didn't know what to say. Guilt pressed down on my shoulders. I couldn't keep pushing him away like this, but inside I was conflicted. I didn't want to stop, but I wasn't prepared. All the things he'd just told me were in my mind along with my dad's cautionary words, and the last thing I wanted was to mess up my plans or prove his stupid dad and brother right.

Finally he exhaled and sat up. "I'm sorry."

I tried to laugh, but it sounded weak. "No, I'm sorry." I stood and dusted the sand off my bottom. "I need to get ahead of us." My legs were wobbly, and I wouldn't dare look into his eyes.

"It's my fault." He stood and pulled the tee back over his head.

I reached forward and laced our fingers, pulling him toward the house. "It's late, and my parents don't know I'm here. I'd better go."

We walked back in silence, me trying to find the right words to say, to explain how I was feeling. But nothing was coming. "Your family is pretty screwed up. But you seem okay."

He laughed. "Appearances can be deceiving."

We stopped at my car, and I looked up at him. "They're not so deceiving. In all of it, you've just been looking out for your family. That's good."

"Maybe," he looked down. "Look, I knew all the way back at the beginning it was too much—"

"Stop!" That hint of desperation was back. "I meant it when I said it doesn't matter to me. I mean, it does, but I don't care about that. I mean... I just... I wasn't ready. I wasn't... prepared."

He nodded, but I wasn't sure he understood. "It's okay," he said. "We'll talk soon."

A brief hug and he stepped back toward the house. I drove home feeling better and worse than when I'd arrived. I knew so much about him now, and it was wonderful. And terrible. I tried to imagine him being expelled for beating someone, needing anger management. Maybe Dad was right, and I was wrong. Maybe Jack was dangerous.

Things had gotten so complicated so fast. Still, I

could never say he didn't warn me. I sighed. Jack was just so totally hot and sexy and exciting. I was determined to ride this one out. Everything in me felt like I didn't have a choice. I wanted to be with him and be a part of his life so much. It made me feel exciting, and a little glamorous, too.

Crossing the narrow strip of land that separated his world from mine, the waves seemed agitated as they crashed on the shore. The moon was hidden behind a large mass of clouds, and I could see lightening flicker purple in them every so often. The orange streetlights shone in rippling circles on the black water, and I wondered what I'd be doing right now if Gabi were still here and I hadn't gone to the beach that day.

I couldn't even imagine.

Chapter 9

The next week drove me crazy between Jack's continued silence and my obsessing over what it might mean. I decided to take Julian up on his offer to visit his studio. I'd never made it over while working on the story, and he was always a good distraction.

It was like a sauna in the small garage, and Julian's shirt was off. The hot wax method of jewelry-making was very delicate and involved setting tiny shells in wax molds and then filling the molds with sterling silver. Once he had made a series of tiny silver shells, he started the task of soldering them together into a ring.

It was fascinating work, but as I watched him, studying the lines on his torso, I was distracted by how much he reminded me of Jack on the sailboat that day. It wasn't just their similar build, but his movements and his focus. It was odd. If I just looked at Julian's body, I'd swear it was Jack.

Or more likely, I was going crazy with missing my... whatever Jack was. I glanced up and caught Julian's eyes on me.

"Were you just checkin me out?" He stood up straight, eyes slanted.

"No!" I answered too fast.

Julian grinned, pointing his torch at me. "You were checkin me out."

I felt my cheeks turning pink. "I was not. I was thinking about Jack."

He frowned and bent down again to continue working. "Where is the golden boy anyway?"

"His brother's in town, so he's been at home. Didn't Lucy say anything about it?"

"Nah. She doesn't talk about them."

"What do you guys talk about?"

"Art. What I do... I guess me mostly."

She knows what boys like. "You really like her?" I asked.

Julian shrugged. "She's cool, I guess."

He stopped and pushed his goggles back to examine the ring. I was sitting on a nearby bench holding a welder's lens in front of my eyes to protect them from the white-hot light.

"Have you taken it up a notch?" I asked, wondering why I even cared.

He glanced at me. "No. We're taking it slow."

"Well, I love the ring. She's going to be thrilled when she sees it. Of course, if she's not, I'll be happy to take it off your hands."

"I'll keep that in mind."

"So what's the status on art school? Have you applied or what?"

He pulled off the goggles and grabbed a shirt, pulling it on as he spoke. "I'm building my portfolio now. I'll probably make another piece like this to put in it, and then I have to go for an interview. Mom and I are going to drive over and tour the campus during spring break, and one of the galleries has offered to write me a recommendation and show some of my smaller pieces in their collection. And I've got your story now. Thank you."

"Wow. I'm impressed. You're really on top of things."

"Didn't think I had it in me?" He grinned.

"Of course not. It's just, you're always joking around and stuff. But not with this. You're so serious."

"What other choice do I have?"

I nodded and he picked up a cloth and started polishing the ring.

"What do you think about Lucy's dad?" I asked, watching him. "Have you met him? Or her brother William?"

"No, I pretty much stay away from those guys. I doubt they'd think too much of me with Lucy." He held the ring up to look at it again. "You're going to the party, right?"

"Honestly?" I studied my Chucks. "I haven't been invited."

"What?" Julian frowned.

"Jack hasn't mentioned it, and I'm not sure if it's because he doesn't want me there or they don't want me there or if he thinks Lucy invited me..."

Julian turned and sat beside me. "You could ask him."

"Well, that's weird. I mean, what? Invite myself to his party?"

"I could ask Lucy about it."

"Would you?" I jumped around to face him. "Oh, Julian, that would be perfect. But don't make it sound like I put you up to it, okay? Just say something like you didn't think I'd gotten an invitation or something."

"I gotcha covered," he chuckled. "I never forget a favor."

* * *

Back home, I jogged up the stairs to my room. I took a deep breath and fell back on my bed forcing my fingers into my hair as my heart tried to settle down. I exhaled loudly but still felt like I was having trouble breathing. Alone again, I was so anxious. I didn't want to think about anything except Jack and why he wasn't calling and what I could do about it. What if he'd decided I was too inexperienced? What if he just didn't need any more trouble?

I was losing it, and I needed to hear a friendly voice. I flipped over to my stomach and grabbed my phone and the notebook where I'd scribbled her new number. I'd never even saved it. I tapped it out quickly and listened to the ring tone.

"Anna?"

Hearing my best friend's voice, I had to struggle not to burst into tears. "Gabi? Oh, Gabi!"

"You finally called," she laughed. "You weirdo. What have you been doing? How are you?"

"Terrible!" I choked out a laugh. "Come back now!"

"You know I can't do that. What's going on? What's so terrible?"

Her voice completely distracted me from my pain. "No, you first. How's Key West? Do you like it? Have you met any celebrities?"

"Um… no," she laughed again. "But Key West is gorgeous. It really is beautiful. And there are chickens everywhere! And cats with thumbs."

"What?" I felt giddy, and I laughed, too.

"And everyone here has five jobs. I swear the guy who helped us at the airport was the same guy bagging our groceries at Fausto's. It's like one of those old television shows where the same person keeps popping up in a different outfit." I laughed and she kept going. "Now what's so terrible?"

"You're going to hassle me, but I met this guy. And oh, Gabi, he's so hot."

"Oh my god! You're in lu-uv."

I giggled again. "Well, I'm definitely in pain now, so maybe I *am* in love. I don't know."

"Who is he?"

"Jack Kyser? His sister is Lucy, and she's just beautiful, too—"

"Kyser? Like the people who own East End Beach?"

"Oh my god," I cried. "You are so my mom. They don't own East End Beach. Their dad just did a lot of the development down there."

"No hassle here—I'm impressed! So you're going out with him? What's that like. Those guys are super rich."

"Well, I sort of was. But then it didn't work out. His dad came up and was really mean to me, and I left and then Julian asked me to the Back to School dance. So I actually went with Julian."

"Wait, you went to a dance with Julian? *My* Julian?" she shrieked. "I can't believe it. Traitor!"

"He was never your Julian," I defended myself. "And it was just as friends. But while we were there, I started talking to Jack again, and he ended up bringing me home."

"And then the make-out began?"

"Oh, god, yes. His shirt was off, and his hands were... everywhere. It was so hot."

Gabi squealed. "Was it on the beach?"

"Yes."

She squealed again. "Okay, so what's the problem?"

"He's just pulled away. His older brother came into town, and now they're talking about him starting college in the spring, and I'm afraid it's just... over."

My stomach ached saying the words.

"Did you call him?"

"Yes! I even went over there to see if he was okay, and oh, god. Did I say his dad was mean? His brother is even meaner."

"What's wrong with these people?" I loved my defensive friend.

"I don't know."

A moment of silence, and then Gabi switched into problem-solving mode. "Okay, press pause and let's think about this. You've snogged. He's got Satan at his house. Give the boy a break. He'll call you. You know how guys are. They like totally go all inward when life gets hard."

"I guess so," I said. "I just miss you. It would be so great if you were still here. Then we could do something, and I wouldn't have to just sit here and think about it all the time."

"I know."

We were quiet again, and I imagined my friend beside me twirling a curl or flipping through a magazine. "Miss you," I said.

"Miss you, too, Banana-face."

"That's another thing. Dad stopped calling me that when he's around."

"Well, that's not being true to you," Gabi laughed.

"It is. I have never liked that nickname."

She snorted some more. "Hang in there. And don't wait so long to call next time."

"Okay."

I felt degrees better after talking to Gabi. I was lying back on my bed thinking about her advice when the phone rang again in my hand. My heart flew into my throat. Maybe it was Jack. I held it up. Julian. Must be about the party.

"Hey, Julian, what's up?" I said.

I could barely hear his voice, and I sat up fast. Something was wrong. He was shouting over background noise. "Julian?" I said again.

"There's been an accident—it's Lucy. She took something, and... I don't know what, but she's unconscious. I need you to go to the hospital in Fairview. And bring Jack."

The line went dead, and I couldn't think. Jumping out of the bed, I grabbed my purse and the keys, shouting to Mom that I'd be back. As I ran, I punched in Jack's number, but of course it went to voicemail.

"I don't know when you'll hear this," I said, "Julian just called. Get to the hospital in Fairview. Lucy's had an accident."

Chapter 10

The drive to the hospital took less than ten minutes, but it felt like ten hours on the small, two-lane county road leading into town. I gripped the steering wheel the whole way, wondering if Jack would get my message and what to do if he didn't. Perhaps I was headed in the wrong direction, and I should've gone to his house. All I'd been thinking about was the fear in Julian's voice and getting to him.

Finally I reached the hospital, dashed through the automatic doors and went straight to the information desk.

"I need the room number for Lucy Kyser," I said.

"She's in the ICU," the woman said. "They're not allowing visitors at this time."

But I was gone as the words were still being spoken, around the corner and down to the next wing scanning each wall plaque for directions to intensive care. As I approached, I saw Julian sitting in one of the chairs that lined the hallway. He looked up and stood as he saw me practically running to him.

"What happened?" I reached out to hold his hand.

He pulled me close. "We'd been drinking, and she had some pills." He was speaking quietly. "She went into the bathroom, and a few minutes later I heard a crash. I couldn't wake her up..."

Before he'd finished speaking I heard the voice I'd spent the last week dreaming about. My stomach clenched, but tonight the sound was completely different, low and furious.

"What did you do to her?" Jack strode down the hall, and the look in his eyes reminded me of both his dad and William times ten. It was like I didn't even know him.

"Jack, stop. It's not Julian's fault—"

"What was it?" His voice grew louder, and he grabbed the front of Julian's shirt. Even though my heart was flying, I jumped in between them pulling on Jack's arm.

"Jack! Stop it! You're going to get us kicked out of the hospital."

"Nothing, man. I didn't do a thing." Julian's voice was flat, and he pushed Jack's hand away, leaning back and sitting down in the chair again.

Jack didn't even speak to me. He only turned to the small room where Lucy was being held. I followed him slowly, stopping at the door as he went inside and approached the bed. There were beeping sounds and tubes running to her arms. He pulled a chair to sit beside her, and her eyes fluttered open, a weak smile touched her lips.

"Lucy," he whispered as he took her small hand in both of his. My stomach hurt when I heard the tear in his voice, and my own eyes warmed.

The door eased shut, and I went over to where Julian was leaning forward in his seat. I sat beside him and put my arm across his shoulders, pressing my cheek into the one closest to me.

"Julian. I'm sorry." I said, rubbing his back. "He's just upset."

"This isn't going to work, Anna."

"Shh," I whispered, still rubbing his back.

"I mean, you know I'm not into drugs, and if she's trying to kill herself..."

We both braced when we heard the loud voice of Mr. Kyser down the hall.

"Where is she?" His voice was stern, but I detected a note of fear, too.

Julian stood. "I'm taking off."

A nurse quickly approached and took Mr. Kyser's arm, leading him to the station in the center of the hall.

"Tell her I said 'bye. I'll catch up with her tomorrow," Julian said.

I nodded, and he left as Bill Kyser strode toward me, eyes blazing.

"Is her brother in there?" he demanded.

"Yes, sir." My whole body was tense with fear. How did he know if Jack hadn't told him? I was pretty sure Julian wouldn't call Bill Kyser. I wasn't even sure if they'd ever met.

He paced the floor and looked at his watch several times. A shudder passed through me, and I sat in the chair again, hugging my arms around my knees. Finally, Jack came out of Lucy's room. His demeanor was back to controlled like always, the momentary glimpse of his other side gone. I stood to go to him.

"She's resting," he said. "I think we need to give her some time."

"Time?" His father snapped. "I'm about to give her an ultimatum. This nonsense has to stop. Just like her mother." He turned his back to us, and I saw Jack flinch.

He put his hand on his father's arm. "This is a lot more than nonsense."

The edge was back in Jack's voice, and Mr. Kyser met his gaze. At first I thought there might be an argument. A bad one. But instead his father broke away.

"I'll be at my office," he said.

The small hallway seemed very still after he left, and Jack looked at me with tired eyes. I still felt shaky, but I went and put my arms around him, pressing my cheek to his chest. He wrapped his arms around me and placed his lips on the top of my head, inhaling.

"Why can't she see that the older we get, the easier it'll get?" He exhaled.

"I don't know." I didn't. This was all new to me. Like everything since I'd met Jack. "Will she be okay?"

"Maybe. Probably." He shook his head. "Thanks for calling."

"I've missed you," I said my voice thick, my heart in my throat. Maybe it wasn't the time, but I had to tell him.

"Me, too. We'll talk soon, okay?"

His words made my stomach hurt. It was over, I could tell by the tone in his voice, and I was sure he was trying to figure out how to let me down easy. I nodded and watched him re-enter Lucy's room before I turned to go.

Chapter 11

Mom had left early for work the next day and being alone in the house was simply too much. I was exhausted and worried, and I decided to head over to Julian's before school. He was in his studio holding a piece of scrap metal when I got there, and he looked like he hadn't slept either.

"Hey," I said. "You staying home today?"

His face relaxed when he saw me, and I went over to hug him. He stood, folding me in his warm embrace, and I held him for a several moments, feeling myself finally calming down. I took in a deep breath of ocean air, and with my eyes closed, it was hard to tell who was comforting whom. It felt really good, and I was sad when we let go.

"Sorry for scaring you like that," he said. "Your number was the only one I could think to call."

I rubbed his shoulder as we sat beside each other. "Are you kidding? I'm glad you called. I can't imagine what you were going through."

"I never thought she'd do something like that."

"What happened?"

"She called and wanted to come over, so I said sure." He looked down, rubbing his thumb across the little dragonfly on his hand. "She was real upset talking about her father and William and how they were forcing her to graduate and move to New Orleans. I guess it was wrong, but she looked like she needed a drink. Brad left his fifth from the other night, so we polished it off. Then she started talking about us running away together."

He stood and walked to the other side of the garage looking out. The sky was grey and the wind had picked up. "She was saying crazy shit. I thought she was joking. I told her I wasn't running anywhere."

"It's not your fault," I said, going to him. "She's just, well, she's been through a lot, you know?"

"She'd already taken something, more of whatever it was before she got here. I didn't know or I wouldn't have let her drink so much," he looked at me, and I hated the pain in his eyes. "I'm sorry for her, Anna. I don't want her hurting, but I can't fix what's wrong in that house. And I can't risk my plan on shit like this."

He looked down again, and I could tell he was still processing.

"You did the right thing, though. You got her help, and I could see you were worried about her."

"I like Lucy. But we've never even been on a real date. I've never been to her house. When she called last night, I was actually thinking of…" His eyes flickered to mine.

"What?" I frowned.

"I just had other things on my mind."

I nodded. We leaned against the door, watching the storm roll in. The air smelled heavy with rain. He let out a deep breath, and after a few minutes, he propped his wrist on my shoulder.

"Thanks for coming. Last night, today."

"Couldn't let my favorite artist suffer alone," I smiled.

"Suffering's good for art." He stood up and walked to the back of the garage.

"What'll you do today?" I asked.

"I don't know. Head down to the water. Might as well take advantage of the weather."

"I hate it when you surf in this. It's so dangerous."

He hauled out his board, grinning, and walked back to where I was standing. "I'll be fine. It's the only time the waves are big enough to ride. You'd understand if you'd let me teach you."

I looked out at the sky. It was getting really grey. "I'd better go or I won't beat it. Call me if you need anything."

"Okay."

But before he left, he stopped and leaned the board against the garage beside me, pulling off his shirt. "Hey, Anna?" He gently put both hands on my shoulders, and I looked up at his stormy eyes. "Let me know if things don't work out with him, okay?"

Nobody knew what Jack had said to me last night, and I hadn't wanted to talk about it. I started to argue, but Julian's hands moved from my shoulders to my cheeks, and he leaned down to kiss me softly on the lips. It was a simple kiss, much like the one he'd given me in class, but unlike that day, this time I couldn't seem to break away from it. My reaction was completely unexpected. I didn't feel afraid or desperate or like I was trying to keep up. I felt warm and good, and I wanted to clutch his shoulders and pull him closer.

Instead, I put my hand on his chest and made myself step back. "Julian—"

"Shh." He put his finger on my lips and smiled. Then he turned, grabbed his board, and walked out the door, down the few blocks to the Gulf. I stood alone watching him go, my eyebrows pulled together as I tried to figure out what had just happened and what it meant.

I could still feel his hands touching my cheeks, his lips softly pressing against mine. That quiet hum was still running through my body, and I hugged my arms over my chest. My brain was just confused. Only a few days ago I'd thought how much Julian reminded me of Jack. My involuntary reaction to his kiss was simply the result of my inner concern about Jack and his family. It was all very logical. Like math or something.

Still, I shivered as I walked to my car, heading quickly to class before it was too late.

* * *

The news of what had happened with Lucy hadn't made it to school, and I hoped with the Kyser's level of control, it never would. It didn't seem fair to her with only a very few having the whole story. My thoughts were still swirling around all that had happened when my English teacher stopped me in the hall. She had a frown on her face, and I had no idea what I'd done. I'd managed to make it before the bell, so it couldn't have been my second tardy.

"Miss Sanders, I received an email from Curtis Waters, the publisher of Coastal Connection News. They need a student intern to help them maintain their Internet site and perform some other duties in the Fairview office. You're my best writer, so I recommended you for the job."

My eyes flew wide. I couldn't believe my ears. An internship with the city newspaper was like the golden ticket to journalism school! Not only that, Coastal Connection owned papers in several towns in South County. It would be an incredible addition to my résumé.

"Oh! Thank you!" I tried not to squeal. "What do I need to do?"

"First you have to get your parents' permission," she drilled. "Then you'll have to make an appointment for an interview with Mr. Waters."

"Of course! I'm sure my parents will be thrilled. Should I call him? Is there an application for me to fill out?"

"I told him you would stop by and pick up an application after school today. Unless Mr. Kyser will be taking up too much of your time." She was still frowning, and I almost laughed, my emotions were so mixed up.

"I'll be there!" is all I said.

* * *

Curtis Waters looked like every news editor I'd ever seen in the movies. His mostly grey hair was in need of a trim, and he wore a yellowed button-down shirt that was intermittently untucked from where he'd jammed it into his khaki pants earlier in the day. He smelled faintly of cigarette smoke, and his wrinkled face was the texture of thick leather. When we met, he was sitting behind his desk leaning back in his chair. He glanced at my application and then up at me and then back at my application again.

I had run home and changed into my best newspaper-reporter outfit before coming—khaki skirt, white oxford, loafers. My hair was tied back in a neat ponytail, and I tried to project confident news-reporter vibes as he appraised my lack of experience.

He continued looking at my half-sheet résumé, and I wondered if this was part of the interview process, seeing if I would crack under pressure and run from his office in tears. If only he knew what my last few weeks had been like.

And I was too excited for such behavior. I'd watched enough old newspaper movies to know he could be my hard-boiled boss ready to bust my chops if I misquoted someone or got a story wrong. I wanted to be tough, able to take it. The truth was, he actually looked like a nice guy.

"You're the one who wrote that feature about the metal arts kid? LaSalle?" He pulled a piece of paper from one of the many stacks around his office.

"Yes, sir."

"I got that," he frowned. "Kid's good. He'll end up doing something. Alex LaSalle's son."

"Yes, sir," I said brightly.

"Humph." He read some more. "You know newspapers are dying. Technology, tree huggers, soon there won't be any local paper left. What do you think about that?"

"I-I guess we'll find another way to get the news out?" I flinched at my dumb response. I hadn't prepared for that question.

"Another way. When the corporate paper came in, they said our little mullet wrappers would be gone inside a year. But folks around here are dedicated. Our circulation took a hit, but Fairview, Coopersdale, Newhope, they're our biggest markets. Loyal customers. And now those corporate guys are gone."

"Yes, sir." My brow creased. Was that the right answer?

"You'll learn a lot working here," he continued. "I want you to feel free to ask me anything you need."

"Yes, sir."

"I'm putting you on our Internet news and the desk. Do you type?"

"Oh, yes, sir."

"You won't have to do much typing. You'll take the published stories off the server and repost them to the website. Clean 'em up a little, take out odd spacing, add bylines. It's pretty simple stuff. Open the mail, check email. If anything looks newsworthy, pass it along to the editors. Scan faxes and type up phone calls, and send them through email."

"Yes, sir." I was starting to feel like a broken record, but I wasn't about to say no.

"You'll be working after school?"

"Yes, sir."

"Put in five hours a week, and I'll pay you a hundred bucks a month."

My eyes widened at that. "Thank you!"

"You'll work in this office, out there." He pointed to a small desk that had an ancient computer buried under assorted papers. "Start next week."

I was so excited, I ran to the Kia and punched up Mom's number. "I'm in! I'm working for the paper in Fairview! He wants me to start next week, five hours a week, and he's going to pay me a hundred bucks a month! Isn't that great?"

"Um…" She didn't sound impressed.

"MOM! Internships are usually unpaid!"

"Oh, well, in that case, yes! It's great," she laughed. "Your first paying gig."

"I'm not really writing. I'm just copying the printed stories to the website and forwarding emails that I think look newsworthy." Then I panicked. "How do I know what's newsworthy? I've never worked at a paper before. What if what I think is newsworthy isn't what

Mr. Waters thinks is newsworthy? He's going to fire me!"

"Sweetie, you haven't even started," Mom said. "Don't can yourself so fast. I'm sure he's not expecting you to be a whiz right off the bat."

"He had my feature on Julian." I thought about how that story had made every paper in South County — and Sterling, the next county over. It had been as much a thrill for me as for Julian.

"Did he say it was brilliant?"

"No, but he had it, and he said he looked at it." I was starting the car, excited about my own portfolio now. "They all ran that one, so I guess it shows I have a nose."

"You have a very cute little nose."

"Mom! Reporters are not cute. They're hard-boiled and cynical."

"You have to live a little longer to be so cynical."

"I've watched a lot of old movies," I said, directing the car toward the beach road. "I know about the evil that lurks in the hearts of men."

"What did you just say?"

I started giggling, "I don't know!"

We both laughed then, and I hung up.

Chapter 12

My euphoria over my new gig was dampened only by my concern for what was happening with Lucy. I'd considered going by the hospital, but it was more likely she was already home. I hated thinking of her in that house with only one person there for comfort. Who knew what the other two would say to her.

I wasn't sure if I should call or text her or if her phone would even be on, and without really considering the possibilities, I turned the wheel and drove the distance to their mansion on Peninsula Avenue. My nerves vibrated in my chest as I knocked on the side door, and I nearly fainted with relief when Jack opened it and then smiled.

"You look very professional." He pulled me through the doorway and planted a kiss on my lips.

So many emotions were rushing through me, I couldn't tell how I felt. His words last night were still in my head along with his tone of finality, but I wasn't ready to question him. I was so happy to see him.

"I had an interview — got a job working at the news office in Fairview."

Eyebrows rose. "Congrats. That's just what you wanted to do, isn't it?"

"Yeah." I smiled as he ushered me into the house. "At least for now. It's the right field and everything. But how's Lucy? Can she have visitors? Would she want to see me?"

"I think that'd be great," he said. "She's less down today. Rachel sent over some flowers, and she'd probably like to see a friendly face."

I wasn't surprised Rachel had heard the news—more that she hadn't said anything to me about it. But I'd been distracted all day with everything that had happened. Jack led me upstairs to Lucy's bedroom. It was the first time I'd seen it, and I was amazed at how beautiful it was.

The entire second level of the house was floored with heart pine, and Lucy's room had the same on her vaulted ceilings. The walls were painted a soft golden hue, and the furniture was dark mahogany. Her bed was piled high with pillows and Battenberg lace, and a beautiful Edwardian armchair with a pretty shell design was beside it. I sat there and reached for her hand. Jack slipped out of the room.

"How are you feeling?" I asked.

"Like a complete idiot," she said without emotion.

I chewed my lip, unsure how to respond. So I just stroked the top of her hand and looked down at it.

"Have you talked to Julian?" she asked.

I nodded. "He wanted me to tell you he waited at the hospital, but when your dad showed up, he had to go."

"Oh, god, I'm so embarrassed," she moaned covering her face with both hands. "Would you please tell him I'm sorry?"

"Sure, only I don't think he expects…"

She clasped my hand. "I just wanted to escape for a little while. You know? I didn't mean for anything bad to happen. It was just supposed to make me feel relaxed, but I guess after a few drinks—"

"You could've died," I said softly.

"I know," she breathed, releasing me. "Would you just tell him… please just tell him I said sorry."

"You could tell him."

"No," she said and looked down. "I can't see him again. After what all I said, it would be too... humiliating. I'd just really appreciate it if you'd tell him I'm sorry for all of it."

I nodded. "Jack says you'll be back at school in a week."

"Like it matters. We'll be gone by Christmas."

My stomach plunged at those words. *Gone by Christmas...* I took a breath and tried to keep my focus on comforting her. "Still, you have friends, right? And —"

"Oh, Anna, what am I going to do? I can't move to New Orleans. I don't want to live with William." Her voice cracked, and tears filled her eyes.

My chest ached seeing her so broken, and I hated knowing they were definitely leaving. "Do you have to go?" I tried. "I mean, what if you came up with a different plan? Something that would keep you here, but give you something to do?"

"Like what? Nothing interests me, I don't know about the business. I'm not good at anything."

"That's not true!" I said. "You're very smart. I've seen you in action, and you're a whiz in civics. Maybe you could work in government... or law."

"I don't care about law."

"Well, I mean, maybe you don't care about much of anything right now. But after you've had some rest, you might feel differently. And as beautiful as you are and as much money as you have, you could do whatever you wanted! What about fashion or design? You could go to New York..."

"Alone?"

I took a deep breath. I was not helping at all, and I wasn't surprised. I was miserable now, too, and I had no idea what I was talking about. She probably needed professional advice, not words of ignorance from inexperienced me. I was having trouble controlling my own feelings these days. So I tried a different approach.

"My mom told me one time that when I started high school she felt like her life was over and no one needed her anymore," I said. "That's when she started volunteering at the arts association, and it's made all the difference in the world for her."

"Volunteering?" Lucy frowned.

"Sure. I know the Haven is always looking for someone to walk dogs." It probably wasn't the sexiest suggestion, but it was the first thing that popped into my head. And it was dogs, right? They were supposed to make you feel better, weren't they?

"Dog walking?" Lucy was skeptical.

"I don't know. I don't know anything except you're my friend, and I hate to see you like this."

She reached for my hand. It was the first time I'd been around her that she wasn't laughing with each sentence or simply effervescent. And I wanted to tell her it was okay. She was safe to have dark days, too. And not to panic, it would pass. I thought it was something her mother might say if she were here. But I didn't know.

"I'm sorry if I've made you feel worse," I said.

"You came to see me." She smiled a little, and I knew she was trying to let me off the hook.

"I'll come again if you want, and I'll help you brainstorm ideas. You could do so many things. People like you, Lucy. Everybody likes you."

She nodded. It was what she'd said to me that first night when she'd wanted to set me up with Jack.

"Right," she said.

* * *

I left Lucy's side feeling like a total failure. Jack came out of what had to be his room, and our eyes met. Without a word, I went to him. His bedroom was large like Lucy's, but instead of lace and golden yellow, it was dark, marine-blue stripes with the same dark mahogany furniture. Books were scattered around the floor and a few college catalogs were stacked on his corner desk. A picture of him looking about ten years old, sitting on a boat and wearing a big grin was on a bookshelf. It made me smile. I'd missed him so much.

Music was playing quietly, and I felt him behind me. His arms slid around my waist, and he put his chin on my shoulder. My heart beat faster, and I turned to pull his face to mine. Shoulders tense, I kissed him, thinking of his words, Lucy's words, what I knew was coming. He was still holding me, gently rubbing my back, when I moved to look at him again. Messy golden hair fell into his clear blue eyes. It seemed unfair that I had just started to know him and now it was ending.

"Thanks for coming to see her," he said. "She's talking to a counselor. We hope that'll help."

I nodded, my eyes traveling over his face.

He stepped away from me then and cleared his throat. It was like he was preparing himself, growing distant by degrees. "When I said we needed to talk last night, I wanted to explain why it's best if we don't... you know." He looked away, over my shoulder, and exhaled. "This is harder than I thought."

"Are you ending it?"

His eyes returned to mine, and he nodded. "I really like you, Anna, and the few times we've been together, I thought we could have fun. Make some memories. But now —"

"That's what I want, too!" I hated sounding so needy, but I couldn't help it. I still wasn't sure how I'd managed to end up here, but I wanted to stay — at least a little longer. "Can't we try? You'll still be here a few more months."

"I don't know," he said. "I don't know if that's fair to you." He tried to step away, but I caught his arms, pulling him to me.

"It can be."

He leaned down to kiss me, and I kissed him back hard, putting everything I had into it. I wasn't thinking about logic or preparedness; I only wanted to keep him. I was willing to take a chance, move faster, if it would get me more time.

His hands were at my waist, and I helped him untuck my shirt. He stepped back to sit on his bed, and I went to him, sitting on his lap, facing him in a straddle. I held his cheeks and kissed him again. Our mouths opened, tongues entwined, and he cupped my butt, lifting me hard against his body. My hands traveled down to his shirt, loosening the buttons and tracing my fingers on his warm skin. His mouth left mine briefly to exhale a low murmur of satisfaction against my neck. It was hot and electric very encouraging.

He held me, rocking me against his body, and I kissed his face, a scratch of stubble brushing my lips. I kissed his mouth. It was softer, and I slipped my tongue inside, tasting a little bit of mint as he continued gently moving us together. I cupped his cheeks and my fingers traveled to his hairline as our mouths explored each others', our bodies still moving together. I started to understand what was happening as heat unfolded low in my stomach, tightening through my core. My focus shifted, and I joined the motion, rising on my knees against him. I was less gentle, increasing the pace as the pressure built and our tongues crashed together. My pulse beat fire under my skin, and my fingers were gripping his back now. All my focus was centered on the point where our bodies met, moving against each other. I gasped between kisses, little noises coming from my throat. *Don't stop, don't stop,* echoed desperately through my brain as the tightness grew so strong, I thought I would implode.

All at once, it burst through my legs, and a breathy cry flew from my mouth. Jack kissed my neck, and I held onto his shoulders, pulling him closer as the sensation pulsed through me. His hand slid under my skirt, and a thumb pressed inside, prompting another, lower noise from my throat. He covered my mouth, still burning kisses along the side of my neck to my ear, his breath tickled in my hair. My aching eased with his touch, but my heart still beat so hard. I'd never made out with a guy that way. It was amazing and intense.

I rested my head on his shoulder, trying to steady my breathing, holding onto the shimmery feeling. I felt like things had to be different now. My hands were still under his shirt, and I caressed his skin, feeling the firm muscles there, as he hugged my waist.

He tilted my head up and kissed me like he was taking a sip of water. "Good?" he whispered.

I nodded, my eyes still closed. His hands massaged my waist again, and I leaned in for another round of kisses. If that was the warm-up, I knew what was coming next. And I wasn't going to stop it this time. But just as my hands slid lower on his stomach, a door slammed downstairs followed by the sound of voices.

We both tensed.

Jack took a deep breath and caught my cheeks, kissing me two more times quickly before helping me off his lap and standing. He crossed the room to open his door, and I stood, straightening my clothes.

I went to him at the door, and he lightly touched my face, a sad smile in his eyes. "Breaking up is hard," he said.

"But, wait... I don't understand. You're still ending it?"

He nodded, but I just blinked. I couldn't believe it. He couldn't mean that—it didn't make sense. I followed him out, studying his perfect body, his straight posture as we walked down the stone staircase. I was still a little wobbly and very confused when we reached the large living room. Mr. Kyser stood in front of the massive fireplace.

I froze, then I whispered, "I left my bag in Lucy's room."

"I'll get it," Jack said, running back up the stairs, leaving me alone with his father.

I tried to be as small and quiet as possible and made my way to the bar area to wait, hoping to go unnoticed. Mr. Kyser had his back to me, and he appeared to be deep in thought, staring at a picture on the mantle. I looked down at the beige stone floor.

"They were three when their mother died," he said, breaking the silence. "My business was really taking off, and I didn't know what I was going to do. Will was eight, so he was in school."

My eyes went back to him, but I didn't respond. I didn't know how to, and he continued speaking.

"Their grandmother came to stay with us. I was working practically around the clock, so I never saw her.

Or them. I didn't want to. I was hoping I would wake up, and it would all be a bad dream."

He turned his cold blue eyes on me, and I felt compelled to say something. "I've never lost anyone close to me."

He looked away. "I'd like to apologize for our first meeting. I was dealing with a difficult situation, and perhaps I'd drunk a bit too much."

I nodded and looked down again. I didn't know how to act around this man. I didn't know what he might say or do. As always in this place, I was in way over my head.

"My daughter likes to get in unique situations," he said. "I think she does it for attention. I'm not sure she realizes that her stunts are very dangerous and not at all funny."

"I think she's sad." I couldn't believe I said it.

"Has she confided in you?"

"No, sir," I said. "I only know when I'm sad, I don't always think about how people around me are feeling and whether the things I'm doing are hurting them. I just don't want to be sad anymore."

"What do you have to be sad about?"

"Nothing like losing my mom," *Or my baby, or having a dad who doesn't like me.* "But my best friend moved away this summer. That was hard."

And whatever just happened with Jack, once the amazement wore off, I was sure I would fall apart.

He turned back to the fireplace, and I decided to swallow my fear and try to help my friend. "Lucy would like it if you talked to her more. She's afraid of what's going to happen after graduation. Maybe you could do something."

"What?" His voice was stern again, and my heart sped up. But I kept talking.

"She didn't tell me this, but I know you have big plans for Jack. You spend every Sunday with him. Do you ever do that with her?"

"Lucy doesn't know a thing about golf. She's only interested in clothes and spa treatments."

"It's not true. She says she's not smart, but she makes good grades. Maybe you could take her out to dinner one night or take her to your office or just try and talk to her."

"We don't have anything to say to each other."

I couldn't believe he was listening to me, and when he looked at me, I could see a little of Jack in his expression. It gave me hope.

"Sometimes conversations just happen. Maybe if you tried—"

"Got it." Jack was back.

Mr. Kyser broke eye contact with me. "I need to return a call," he said and left the room.

Once he was gone, I leaned against the bar and exhaled. I hadn't realized I was holding my breath.

"You okay?" Jack frowned. "What was that about?"

"Nothing," I breathed. "He apologized for that night."

"Good. He needed to apologize."

I looked up at him, my ex- … whatever we were, and he led me out into the growing darkness. I put my hand through his arm, pulling myself closer to him. It was strange. I felt older, like I had turned a corner or learned something new.

He stopped me at the car and placed his fingers on my chin. "Anna Sanders, I'll always remember you."

My brows pulled together. "Are you serious?"

"I have to be." He exhaled and pulled me into a hug. I closed my eyes, breathing in his warm scent. "But I'm glad we got to spend some time together. And I'll be watching for your name in print."

He released me, quickly backing away, and all I could do was frown, unable to answer him. After what just happened—the way he'd kissed me, the way he'd touched me—it all seemed so ridiculously formal. I knew he felt something more, and I couldn't believe he would just walk away from us without even a small fight.

"I'll be watching to see if I believe this," was all I could say.

As I drove home, across the land bridge that separated Hammond from the rest of the island, back to my place in Fairview, I thought of what just happened and tried unsuccessfully to make it make sense.

Chapter 13

Mom was waiting for me when I got home, concern etched on her face.

"I heard there was an incident last night with Jack's sister?" she said. "At the hospital? One of the association members was at the hospital and said the Kysers were there. Is that where you went?"

I decided against telling her the whole story. No use worrying her when it seemed to be under control now. "Lucy had an accident or something. She hit her head and Julian took her in."

"Is she okay? Are you okay?"

"I'm fine, but I'm not sure about Lucy." I sighed, dropping my bag on the counter. "She feels so helpless, and I can't tell if her dad even cares other than to make her stop bothering him."

"That's a pretty harsh thing to say," Mom said, but she only had part of the story.

"He also seems very interested in me not interfering with his plans for Jack." And at this point, he was getting his wish—it was the only reason I could believe. Jack had to be pushing me away because of his dad.

"How in the world could you mess up his plans for Jack? Has he said something to you?"

"Not really." I skipped telling her about the alcohol-birth control quiz. It would just make her mad.

"You know, honey, it's possible Mr. Kyser could be afraid."

"I find that hard to believe."

"Well, think about it. He lost his wife. That can be difficult to get over. And now his daughter gets hurt and winds up at the hospital."

I thought about his words—*Just like her mother.* "Maybe."

"Sometimes adults act as poorly as children."

I went to my room thinking of Mom's words and consumed with everything that had happened in the last three days. After more than a week of nothing, everything happened at once. My college plans got a major boost with my cool new job at the paper, and my personal life exploded, starting with Julian's kiss and ending with Jack saying it was over.

My face heated up when I thought of what I did in Jack's bedroom—what we did. I squeezed my legs together and rolled onto my side, remembering how it felt, his fingers, his mouth. How would I ever be able to forget about him? I couldn't. I didn't want to.

Julian drifted into my mind. He was different, and I was different with him—not desperate. Calm and smart. But my insides didn't work that way. They were torn and obsessed, and I still wanted Jack. He was a bad drug that left me craving more even when it hurt me. Maybe I was the idiot. I was the one swimming with sharks and didn't know it. But how to stop? How did I climb out of the water when everything in me wanted to stay and keep swimming?

* * *

Lucy sent me a text early Saturday morning. *Jack convinced Dad we should still have the party. Julian said you didn't get an invite. Here's one — please come.*

I stared at the words several minutes trying to process two things. Jack still wanted to have their party, and he still hadn't invited me. It hurt, but I was going.

Julian sent me a follow-up text offering a ride within minutes of my receiving Lucy's, and that's how I found myself standing next to him, looking up at the Kyser house, which was lit up and glowing like a crystal palace in the black October night. I'd never seen it this way, and I felt like I was visiting for the first time.

My hair was blown out straight again, but in the white cotton sundress I'd chosen to wear and bronze sandals, I felt like a baby walking up to a house of sophisticates.

"You look great," Julian said. "And Helen Freed better look out for me. I might get better at making her jewelry than she is."

He was dressed in his standard black jeans with a grey blazer over a matching grey tee. With his shaggy, dark locks and rock-star swagger, Julian could pass anywhere—and he seemed at ease everywhere.

"I think everybody'd better look out for you." I was still staring at the mansion. "You're the next big thing."

He threw an arm around my neck and kissed the top of my head. "That's my angel."

The small voice inside me said I should snap out of it. That what I needed was more Julian. But I shut it up. I shoved it far down and away in favor of my body's demand for more Jack. I wanted more of his strange blend of excitement, sex, and intrigue. The life I'd been tossed out of. Maybe.

"What's the plan?" Julian said, interrupting my thoughts. "Party up, then meet at the car around midnight?"

"That's what I told Mom, so yeah. What do I do if you want to stay longer?"

"You can take the T-bird back, and I'll catch a ride with Brad. Don't wreck it." I shook my head as he folded the keys into the sun visor.

As we approached the Kyser home, it seemed wider somehow, with tiny lights illuminating the balconies and guests laughing and spilling over onto the lawn. It was like something out of a movie, only I hadn't been cast in it. Or given the screenplay.

I started to feel nervous about seeing Jack again. I didn't want to seem like a stalker. But Lucy had invited me here. She and I were friends even if he wouldn't give us a chance.

Then I had a worse thought. What if he didn't want me here?

No. I had to believe my non-invite was just an oversight or him trying to protect me. He had to know I would've heard about a party at his house.

Julian sensed my hesitation and pulled my hand through the crook of his arm. But it didn't ease my fear. We were at the door, and my chest was tight, my throat dry. I looked at him wide-eyed.

"Here we go," he said ominously. "Into the lion's den."

Then he laughed and poked me gently in the side as he pushed open the door. It was a different entrance than I'd used before, and from where we stood, I could see inside the house was more decorated than outside. Everything was golden and crystal, and Julian lifted two slim flutes of champagne off a side table as we passed through a waiting room the size of my bedroom. I wondered how many parts of this house I hadn't even seen yet.

We passed through what some people called a mud room, and it had a bench where I supposed you sat to take off your muddy boots after a long day pheasant hunting or something.

"No adults?" Julian whispered, handing me a flute and taking a sip from his. "Is this heaven?"

I glanced at him, and he winked before throwing back the rest of his drink. I followed suit and drained my glass. I might usually avoid alcohol, but tonight was a whole different ballgame.

We passed a bronze half-bath that glowed with golden light. The sink was a large, blown-glass flower, with a brazen stem forming the base. "Cool," Julian pulled away to check it out, but I kept going.

The floors were the same smooth, beige stone apparently throughout the downstairs. Travertine. That's what it was. I recognized it from one of my dad's jobs. Very expensive. Of course.

I passed through the kitchen into the familiar dining and living area with its wall of floor-to-ceiling windows stretching across the north side facing the bay. Another stand of champagne flutes was against the wall, and I took one, quickly sipping to calm my nerves.

French doors opened onto the wrap-around patio made of the same flagstone as the driveway. More kids were spilling out that way, and far across the lawn, I saw Brad and Renee with Lucy. Her dress was a thigh-length, shiny yellow strapless chiffon, and she was radiant and laughing. If I didn't know it, I would never have guessed she was at the hospital two days ago. No sign of her sadness tonight.

Slowly I continued through the house, searching, straining my eyes for him. It seemed like I heard his voice outside, so I made my way to the patio again. But he wasn't there. I kept walking, remembering there was a private balcony around back. Just as I reached the corner, I saw him.

He was standing at the far end looking gorgeous as ever in tailored pants and a light blazer. The perfect host. His blonde hair moved slightly in the breeze, and his lips parted as he smiled. I couldn't help remembering the last time he kissed me, his hands touching me. I wanted to be there, standing beside him, glowing as his date.

But that position had been filled.

My breath caught and instantly my eyes filled. I didn't know her, but she could've been a model. She was as tall as Jack, with short, blonde hair and perfectly white teeth. She was dressed in a sparkly golden slip-dress that moved easily over her lean body. The knot in my throat grew tighter as I watched him say something in her ear, his lips grazing the side of her cheek. She smiled before kissing his mouth and dropping onto the loveseat he stood behind. Just as fast, he took a long drink of amber liquid from a crystal tumbler, and my heart broke as his hand slid down her cheek, past her neck, and into the front of her dress. She dropped her head back, and he bent forward and kissed her.

From far away, I heard the sound of shattering glass. The champagne flute I'd been holding had slipped from my fingers and fallen at my feet. Jack's head lifted and our eyes met. Crystal crunched under my sandals as I backed away quickly, banging into a small table in my haste. I spun around to catch it, and when I looked up, two kids I didn't know were staring at me.

Without a pause, I stood and flew out the back door, running toward the bay. I couldn't see in the darkness. My eyes were still dazzled from the lights of the party and from Jack's betrayal. My stomach throbbed so badly,

I had to get away before the tears started. I knew they wouldn't stop.

I had no idea what I slammed into that threw me to the ground. "Ow!" I cried out, throwing my hands forward as I slid onto all fours.

I only spent a moment on my face. Aching and bleeding, I rose and kept running toward the water, my eyes blurred with tears. I couldn't stop them. Dry-heaves jerked me, until finally I made it to the bay. It felt like someone was jamming a knife into my side. I had a runner's cramp, and I couldn't catch my breath. I dropped onto the sand, gasping and crying. It hurt so bad. I was such an idiot. Such a stupid, stupid idiot, I sobbed.

I didn't remember taking off my sandals, but I was barefoot, lying on my face, clutching the sand in front of me and trying with all my might not to fall apart completely. Not here. But my insides felt like they were being torn out and shredded by a careless butcher, and all I could do was moan as the tears poured from my eyes.

Who was that girl? Clearly, they were very comfortable together. Not even a flicker of hesitation when he felt her up, as if his hands had been there before. That was when I saw the truth. I'd hoped his dad was the reason, but now I knew why he didn't invite me to the party. He didn't want me there.

I coughed, still crying, still fighting tears. I wanted to die. I was so stupid. I wanted to scream and cry. But I had to stop. The smallest note of self-preservation rang in my chest, and I forced myself to get control. It took all my strength, but I pulled myself up and slowly rubbed the sand from my hands and cheeks, taking a careful step on my injured leg. I couldn't go back there, but I couldn't stay here.

My phone was in my purse in Julian's car. Oh god! Julian's car. He'd tucked the keys in the visor, so I could leave when I wanted. I slowly limped up the beach in the direction of the T-bird. I hadn't gone far when I heard a car pull up on the roadside and a door slam.

"Anna? Is that you?" It was Julian.

"Julian? Oh, god." My knees were weak, and I lowered myself again to the sand, tears back in my eyes.

"Jesus, Anna." He jogged to me and knelt at my side. "You totally disappeared back there. I went for drinks and next thing I knew, you were gone. If I hadn't found your shoes... Did you fall?"

"I'm sorry. I... I just—"

"I know. I saw Jack with that Casey chick, and I figured you must be wigging out."

"Casey. That was Casey Simpson?" I asked.

"You know her?"

"No." I whispered, but Lucy's words flooded my brain. She'd broken Jack's heart. Seemed she'd returned to collect the pieces.

"Are you okay?" Julian asked. "Can I do something?"

I looked up at his concerned face. That little voice I kept silencing bleated *yes* with all its might, but I could only cry.

"I'm so stupid, Julian," I sobbed, looking down. "I'm just so stupid. It was all so beautiful, and I wanted to be a part of it. I wanted to be with him..."

"Anna." Julian pulled me into a hug and rubbed my back. My face was cradled warm against his shoulder, but I couldn't stop the sobs jerking me. "Those guys are so messed up. You don't want that."

My voice was muffled against him. "I did. You don't know how much, what I was willing to do."

He took my arms and held me back, looking into my eyes. "You want that life?"

I nodded.

His brow lined. "Then earn it. You're smart enough to have whatever you want. Go out and get it for yourself."

I shook my head and looked down. He didn't understand. I would never be like that.

We sat in silence a few seconds, Julian holding both of my hands. Then finally he gave me a gentle pull. "C'mon," he said, helping me stand. "Let's blow off this party and catch a movie or go to Scoops. This isn't our scene. Over the top, glitzy stupidness for what? A birthday? Acting like nothing even happened two days ago."

"Lucy. What about Lucy? The ring?" I was standing in front of him, our hands still joined.

"I'll give it to you," he smiled, reaching up to move a strand of hair from my eyes. "You liked it, didn't you?"

"You can't give me Lucy's ring." I shook my head, the tears trying to start again. "I just want to go home. Can I just go home now?"

"Sure," he said, holding my cheek. I took a limping step, and he stopped me. "Does it hurt to walk?"

My leg throbbed. I nodded, looking down, and before I realized what was happening, he lifted me in his arms.

"Julian, wait," I held his shoulders. "I'm too heavy!"

He smiled and hugged me close. "Are you kidding? You've seen my sculptures. All that scrap. You're way lighter. And softer."

"Still," I tried to protest.

"It's okay," he said, continuing to walk. I sighed and leaned my cheek against his shoulder. I didn't feel like fighting. Gentle pressure against my temple, and he'd kissed my head. "You'll get over this," I heard him say quietly, under his breath.

We were at the car, and he helped me inside. "Now wait here. I'm gonna go pop that guy in the mouth."

My eyes lifted to his, and I tried to smile back. But my usual return-banter wasn't working tonight. "Please don't."

He pressed his lips together. "Whatever you say."

We drove the whole way back with nothing but the radio playing. My head rested on the seat back, and I studied my savior. His bottom lip moved slightly as he chewed it, and his dark hair was pushed around his face by the open window. He wasn't crowding or questioning me. He was simply taking me home. As I watched him, that little voice inside me whispered, "I love you."

I shook my head and squeezed my eyes closed, trying to remember how many glasses of champagne I'd drunk before finding Jack with his hand down another girl's dress. I would love anyone who helped me right now.

I leaned forward and cranked up the volume, rolling down the windows to let the salty, humid air blow my curls back in.

Chapter 14

By the time I reached home, I was numb, nauseated, and weak. I couldn't stop seeing Jack's hand on Casey's breast or her red lips kissing his mouth. And every time I did, I felt the gut-kicking ache of betrayal all over again.

It made sense now. If I were there, he couldn't be with her, and she'd supposedly run off and left him wanting more. Casey Simpson. She was beautiful and sophisticated and smart. She was in college, and her parents lived on Hammond Island. I was sure his dad had no objections to that match.

I doctored my leg in the bathroom, cleaning off the blood and examining what was already turning into a bruise. Very attractive. I went to my room and crawled under my covers. I didn't think I'd ever get to sleep, but when I opened my eyes again, it was morning. I jumped up and started throwing clothes into my duffel bag. I was getting out of here, and Nana's was the perfect escape.

I was on the beach by afternoon, under an umbrella and nursing my pulverized heart. Nana was working on a project for her Master Gardeners class, so she let me have the day to myself, which was fine with me. I wanted to be alone to suffer.

By sunset, I'd read every article on my tablet, and I'd worked hard to think only about the news and my new job at the paper and not how for a brief time I'd felt like the princess of East End Beach.

And it still hurt.

The sun was setting, and as much as I wanted, I couldn't stay out here forever. I pulled my cover-up around me in the cooling October air, turning just in time to catch sight of him walking up the shoreline in my direction. My breath caught. Jack.

His eyebrows were pulled together, and he was moving quickly toward me. In the space of one second, I went from wanting to scream at him to wanting to cry, to wanting to run to him and kiss him, to wanting to run away or better yet, hit him. He stopped in front of me, looking down as the wind tossed his hair, and my throat was so tight it ached.

"I've been calling you all day," he said, seeming angry. "Your phone goes straight to voicemail. So I called your house, and your mom told me you were here."

Adrenaline vibrated just under my skin, but I managed to say, "Why?"

He let out a deep exhale, dropping to the sand. "I didn't know you'd be there last night."

"I could tell. Your hands were very full."

His blue eyes flashed. "You and I are not together, Anna. And Casey's an old friend."

"An old friend you felt up."

The muscle in his jaw flinched, and he looked out at the water.

"Why are you here, Jack?" I snapped.

He looked back. "I don't know. I was worried about you."

Anger clutched my chest, stronger than the pain in my stomach. It pushed me to my feet. "You don't have to worry about me, Jack Kyser, I'm fine. We're through, and you can do what you want."

He reached for my hand, but I pulled it away, walking furiously down the beach. He ran to catch up and caught my arm, but I jerked it back and kept walking.

"Sure. That's great. Just walk away." His voice was sharp, which only angered me more. "I only came to say I wouldn't have done that to you."

I stopped walking and spun around to face him. "No? You wouldn't? Then what would you do? Kiss me and touch me and leave me wanting more? Then throw me away without any explanation—just in time for your ex to roll into town for a hookup?"

"It wasn't like that." His lips tightened. "And I did try to explain. You have no idea the shit I'm dealing with, Anna. At least she knows what to expect."

The wind was blowing my curls all in my face. He stepped forward and caught a lock in his hand, studying me. "My life. My family. The pressure. It almost killed Lucy... you'll thank me one day."

"I'm thanking you now," I snapped back, pushing his hand away. "And feel free to leave at any time."

"Fine," he said backing up. "I didn't come here to confuse the situation. I just came to apologize. I'm really sorry."

"Yes, you are," I growled. "Apology accepted. Have a nice life."

He paused for a second. Then he stepped forward and caught my cheeks, frustration lining his brow. I wanted to struggle, to push him back hard, but it was too late. He leaned in fast and kissed me, and it was like a flame to gasoline. Heat roared through me and I kissed him back. I was mad and my whole body was tense, but I shoved my fingers into his hair and opened my mouth, pulling him closer, wanting more. His tongue found mine, and I didn't care what happened last night. My legs trembled, and I just wanted him. All of him. I didn't care if it was a huge mistake. I didn't care if it made me weak and pathetic. I hated myself, but my need to have him was stronger than my need to hurt him.

He kissed me two more times, holding my face in his hands then looked into my eyes. "Don't do that."

I was breathing hard. "Do what?"

"I have a reason for ending this." He lowered his hands. "My plans won't change, and us spending time together... You'll just get hurt."

"Why can't you let me worry about that?"

He shook his head. "I won't do that. I like you. You're pretty and smart, and if things were different, well, they would be different. But that's all I can do."

My jaw clenched. I looked down at the sand, and he looked out at the water. He'd pushed me away, and yet here he was apologizing. I was furious, but when he kissed me, none of it mattered. All I wanted was more. He stood here, telling me I didn't understand—and I didn't. All of this was messed up and wrong, and I still wanted him.

"Okay," I said, catching my breath, grasping for anything to make sense. "Explain it to me, then. It's been two weeks since you told me anything. What's going to happen?"

He glanced back at me, and I met his gaze. Then he sighed and looked down.

"I only need two credits to graduate," he said as we slowly started walking back to my stuff. "I don't even have to go every day. I'll take the exams and leave at Christmas. But I'm probably sticking closer. Going to Tulane with Lucy."

I nodded. "That's good."

"I was never into the Ivy League. I'd rather stay near the water, my boat."

His boat. I thought back to the day he'd visited me here, that happy weekend. "I never got my sailing lesson," I said quietly.

He breathed a laugh. "Oh, man."

Even though my chest was still tight, we were both softening. We stood there for a moment, side by side, listening to the water.

Finally he spoke. "I guess I did promise. Name the date, and I'll take you out."

I shrugged. "What about Saturday? I've got to work at the paper all week."

"Right. Good luck with the new job."

I turned and lightly touched his arm. "Thank you. For coming here and apologizing. You could've let it go, but you didn't."

He caught me by the waist and pulled me to him. My hands were on his shoulders, and I was very aware of every place our bodies touched. Then he kissed me, soft lips covering mine. My hands slid behind his neck, his hands slid to my lower back, and the last of my resistance dissolved.

His lips moved to my ear. "You're welcome," he whispered.

He released me and started back across the sand, and as I watched him go, I didn't know what to think. I couldn't figure out any of it—him telling me no and then showing up here today, kissing me like that.

He insisted we couldn't be together, that I'd get hurt. But maybe I could prove him wrong, show him I was strong enough for his family. My lips tightened at the truth. I was no match for Jack's family. I wasn't even strong around him. I wasn't able to fight how my body responded to him, that heat low in my stomach when he kissed me.

But he'd come here because he was worried about me. That had to mean something. Maybe if we kept spending time like this, he would change his mind on his own. Did I want that? I was afraid to commit to an answer with everything in me still humming from his kiss.

Instead, I thought about good journalism schools near the water. I'd never considered Tulane, but maybe I'd do a little research, maybe send them an application. Just to see what would happen—not committing to anything. After all, Lucy and I were friends. She'd probably like it if we were together, and I'd be closer to Mom and Dad.

He was at the top of the dunes when he looked back and waved one last time. I waved, considering my alternate plan.

Chapter 15

I loved working at the city paper. Even if I was only an intern, it made me feel like I was doing something important, moving into my profession, becoming a newswoman. It helped me forget about my silly personal life. Here, I was doing something important, finding the truth, creating a record.

Nancy Riggs, my editor, was a cool boss — very laid-back and easy to work with. The county bicentennial was coming up, and she wanted me to help her collect photographs and old clippings for a big tabloid insert she was planning. She also wanted me to help her with regular flashback features leading up to the event, so part of my job was combing through the archives and pulling old images and stories about South County when there was nothing but farms and dirt roads everywhere. It was amazing to see familiar places looking so primitive, and I was usually in the office way later than I was scheduled to work digging through the dusty old files.

The week passed quickly, and I did my best to avoid bumping into Julian at school. I wasn't sure I wanted to see him after what had happened at the birthday party. Not that I was embarrassed, more I felt the need to put some distance between us for now.

Lucy was thrilled with the ring he'd made her, and she was smiling a little more in class every day. Her meetings with the counselor were helping, she said, and on Saturday, when I arrived for my sailing lesson, she was running around her kitchen buzzy and excited. I was pretty buzzy and excited myself as I put my bag on the counter top. Then I saw she was packing a lunch.

"What's up with the brown bag?" I asked.

"Well, you'll be glad to hear your little speech about volunteering had some unexpected benefits!"

"You're volunteering?" My eyebrows rose. "Where?"

"Months Bay," she said. "They have this program where you can help with dune restoration and get credit. But they do other things—monitoring sea turtle nests, stuff like that. For conservation. I volunteered to help find and label nests."

"Hey, that's cool, and it sounds like fun."

"It is, and guess who else is there earning college credit?" She grinned.

"I have no idea."

"B.J."

I couldn't help laughing. "You found him?"

"It was a total coincidence," she leaned on the bar looking so much like her old self. "He's majoring in marine biology or coastal restoration or something, and he's getting credit for working at the reserve. He's also helping me learn the ropes, and of course I need lots of additional assistance because I'm just having the hardest time remembering directions."

We giggled, but she stopped and frowned, looking at my navy tank, cargo capris, and Chucks.

"What? What's wrong?" I asked.

"First, Skipper, you can't wear those shoes. Only light-colored soles on the boat. And you're going to freeze to death in that tank. I'll loan you one of my windbreakers."

"Thanks, Barbie."

She ran up the stairs and returned with a pair of boat shoes and a nylon hooded jacket.

"See if these fit, and if they do, you can have them. I don't care if I ever sail again."

"Why not?"

She poked out her tongue. "Makes me nauseous. And don't let Jack show off the whole time. Just because he was born on a boat doesn't mean he has the right to annoy you to death with it."

"But... if he was born on a boat, wouldn't that mean you were born..." I teased.

"Figuratively, Anna. That's one gene we do not share."

I smiled and slipped my foot in the shoe. It fit, so I walked out to put my others in the car. Turning back, I saw Jack coming out the door to meet me gorgeous as always and appropriately dressed in a long-sleeved tee and light pants with Sperrys. I was glad I saw Lucy first. He put his jacket in the Jeep and walked over to me.

"Ready to go?" He smiled and my heart beat faster.

I wasn't sure what to expect from today — if it would be just friends or something more. If he was only keeping his word, or if I was even strong enough for this... It was too late now. I had to be.

"Yep!" I said. "And I looked up knots online, so I'm also ready to tie her up!"

We climbed into the Jeep for the short trip to the marina. Before long we were on the crystal blue water, the wind pushing into the tall sails that drove us forward. We put in at Lost Bay headed east, with a plan to sail around the point and back again.

After we'd set a course, Jack went to the rear of the boat and motioned for me to sit beside him. The wind was strong and it was cold on the water, so I sat close to his side.

"I can't believe I didn't go over the safety precautions before," he said. "You might want to consider a better teacher."

"I think you're doing just fine," I smiled, reaching up to smooth the line in his brow. "We were just getting acquainted first trip."

"So you like it?"

"I love sailing!" I pulled my jacket around my bent knees trying to get warmer. "And you've been doing this since you were little? I mean, I saw that picture in your room—you looked ten."

"I was about ten when Dad started driving me to Fairview to do stuff with the yacht club. They let kids join even if their parents aren't members, and they have regattas. Dad was friends with the commodore, and he showed me different tricks. But the best part, which you would love," he said tugging one of my curls, "was the stories, the history of sailing in our area. It's really neat."

"Your dad knows everyone," I said, looking out at the horizon and thinking about his father. "He grew up here, right?"

"Graduated Fairview High School."

"That's so weird. He's so distant now."

Jack shrugged. "He works a lot. And I guess after Mom died, he didn't feel like being involved in the community."

"Do you ever talk about it?" I studied his face. He shook his head, but didn't say more.

I looked away again, searching for a more neutral topic. "My mom said there are pirates around here."

"Well, not in the Sound, but if you go far enough out in the Gulf, you might run into them. I heard a shrimper say he was hit by some around Chandeleur. They took all his catch, his money, gas. He said he was lucky to get away with his boat."

"That settles it," I said. "I'm sticking to the Sound."

"With the big sharks?"

"I don't plan on swimming."

He gave my knee a squeeze and adjusted the tiller to keep us on course.

"So tell me about your boat." I read the name. "*Slip Away*. How long have you had it?"

He stretched back against the seat again. "Well, I'm not really into cars. The Jeep was William's, and I'm fine driving it. I really just wanted a boat. And a micro cruiser's a good size for small groups and shorter trips."

I looked at the shiny wood gleaming in the sunlight. The wind stretching the canvasses made a relaxing sound under the clear blue skies, and even if it was chilly, it was a gorgeous day to be out.

"So you got it what? Two years ago?"

"Yeah. I needed something bigger to take out around here. When I was at the yacht club, we used Sunfish, but they're really too small to do anything other than cruise around in the Bay."

"I don't know what a Sunfish is, but I love *Slip Away*." I shivered.

"A Sunfish is just a dinghy. They're really small. Hey, we can go below if you're getting cold. There's no need to stay up here the whole time. I'll drop the anchor and take a break."

I nodded. He smiled and loosened the mainsail. Then he let the small metal anchor drop into the dark waters. We went down into the small cabin that consisted of a table, a closet bathroom, and a bunk that

137

filled what would be the front of the boat. Tiny slit windows looked out at the water.

"Now you know how to sail," he said. "Promise kept."

I nodded, my thoughts drifting to the bunk and how alone we were. "I'll probably need more practice," I said. "Is this my only trip?"

"I told you I could do this every weekend, so whenever you have time." I watched him slip off his jacket, and I did the same.

"It's cooler than I thought with the wind," I said. "I'm glad Lucy gave me this."

We paused and studied each other for a moment, his eyes flickered behind me and then back to my face. "I'm usually alone out here. It's pretty isolated."

"That's what I was thinking." My stomach was tight, and I took a step closer to him.

But he took a step back. "I'll head up."

"Wait—" I caught his arm and pulled. He didn't need more encouragement.

He held my waist, pulling me closer, and my hands fumbled to his cheeks. Our mouths crashed together, opened, and when our tongues met, a little noise gasped from my throat as that intense heat flared between us.

My eyes were closed, and I barely noticed us fall back on the bunk, me on top with my legs straddling his waist. His hands were under my tank, on my sides, on my bare stomach. He was all around me, warm and ready, and my heart was beating so fast. In that moment, I was so happy. He was into it. He wanted us to be together. I rocked my hips into his, hoping for more of what we'd done in his room, but he caught my cheeks in his hands and held my face above his, looking into my eyes. We were both breathing fast.

"Anna," he said. "I want to do this. But it won't change what I said. We're still not together."

My eyes traveled from his blue ones up to his hair then down to his lips that had just been on mine. My body wanted him, all of him, but reading his expression and hearing his words, I knew it would be a mistake. I released a deep breath as I moved to the side, sitting next to him on the bunk.

He sat up and turned away, running his hands through his hair. I watched as he grabbed his jacket and climbed back up the ladder, then I stepped over to the tiny bathroom and went inside.

The light automatically switched on, and I bent over the sink, commanding myself not to cry. It didn't work. My shoulders folded as tears flooded my eyes. But I inhaled deeply, fighting to stop. I could not fall apart out here with only him. I had to save some dignity.

Several deep breaths, and I turned on the water, letting it run as I studied myself in the mirror, looking deep into my hazel eyes. What did I want? To change his mind? Was that even possible? And was I willing to fight for us when he wasn't even convinced we should try?

I couldn't help my feelings, my desire for him, but I would never change his mind this way. I had to be the one who left him wanting more. Otherwise, I would always lose, and he would always walk away. It would be hard, but I had to be stronger around him. And wasn't that my plan anyway? Stronger around him and his family?

Then maybe, one day, things would be different. Maybe.

I took another deep breath, touched up my face, and went back topside. The anchor was lifted and Jack had repositioned the sails. We were going again, back to the marina. Once everything was secured, he sat in his previous location, and I went back to sit beside him. But this time I didn't get as close as before.

"I'm sorry." I said, trying to project a confidence I didn't feel.

His brow creased. "For what?"

I hesitated. I was sure he knew I meant for coming onto him down below, but I decided not to go there. "I should've been up here helping. That's why I'm here, right? And I never showed you my knots."

He relaxed and leaned forward in his seat. "I'll let you tie her up."

Back at the East End Marina, I attached the boat to the pier with a clove hitch. *The rabbit comes out of its hole, round the tree and back down the hole again.*

He smiled. "A-plus, Skipper."

Once the boat was secure in its lift, we drove back to his house. Standing in the driveway by my car, he stepped forward and gave me a hug. I held him for a moment, my heart clenched, then let him go. "So am I a sailor now or do I need another lesson?"

"You need practice, but I think we'd better put that on hold until the weather changes."

I nodded, wondering if his words had a double meaning.

* * *

Back home in bed, I curled into a ball on my side and let the tears fall. In that moment, I made a vow to myself. From then on, I would be the strong one. No more games and humiliations. No more chasing him. I would focus on school and work and getting back in control. I'd turn the tables before it was all over, and who knew. Maybe one day Jack Kyser would be begging for me.

Chapter 16

As if to help me in my resolve, Jack was taken out of the class we shared and moved into an accelerated independent study. Now I only saw him at lunch when everyone gathered in the quad.

Brad had gotten a brand-new cherry-red Camaro as an early birthday-Christmas present, and it was the talk of the school. I wasn't the muscle car type, but I had to admit it was a slick ride and perfect for him. Rachel was thrilled, and even Julian had seemed impressed when Brad had wheeled it into the student lot.

"We need to see what that baby can do." Julian grinned, clapping hands with Brad as he straddled the concrete bench where we sat having lunch.

"After tomorrow's game, we'll go down to the old beach road, and you can see what driving a new car feels like," Brad said with his usual star-football-player swagger.

Rachel walked up with Renee Barron and the two joined us.

"What's going on?" Rachel asked, sitting down in front of Brad. Jack was with us today as well, but he didn't seem interested in the conversation. I was doing my best not to be interested in him. Time was passing, and though I still missed him, I was keeping my vow.

"The guys want to pit the Camaro against Julian's T-bird after the game tomorrow," I said.

"Won't Julian's car just blow up?" Rachel laughed, but Renee studied Julian.

"Not cool, Blondie. Respect your elders," Julian stood and flipped one of Rachel's locks over her shoulder. "Besides, my car has seen way more action than that new toy."

Rachel frowned, "Did you get overheated in welding, Julian?"

Brad grinned and leaned forward, wrapping his arms around Rachel's waist. "We're catching up."

"I love your car," Renee said in her smooth purr to Julian. They were standing next to each other now, and he put his arm over her shoulder. "And my car loves you. It's been a while."

"Yes it has," she said, moving closer to him. I saw Jack's eyes flick to them and then to me. I looked down at my shoes.

"Well, I'm not planning to race Brad," Julian announced, straightening and shoving his hand in his front pocket. I saw the little dragonfly peeking out. "I was thinking we could take turns test-driving. See who's the biggest puss."

"I'll come," Renee smiled.

"Yes, you will," Julian winked at her, and she laughed, hitting him on the arm. "I'll pick you up for the game."

"I'd like to see that," Jack said, and I studied his face wondering why. He'd almost completely stopped joining us in extracurriculars now. "Go to the game with me, Anna?"

My mouth dropped open, and both Rachel and Renee's eyes flew to me, waiting for my answer. I wasn't super-confident in my "be strong" vow just yet, but I didn't see a way out. I shrugged. "Sure."

"You interested in a race, Silver Spoon?" Brad was super-cocky today, but for once it didn't bother me.

"Jeeps are no match for Camaros," Jack said distracted. I couldn't tell what was on his mind, but he looked at me and smiled. "I'll pick you up and we can go for a few minutes—just to see what happens. And then, whatever you want."

I nodded wondering what that could mean, but I was determined not to be the one starting anything this time. Julian hopped up on the bench and leaned down to touch my nose.

"That cute little nose for news is irresistible," he said. I batted his hand, but I appreciated the save. "Next story you can add professional driver to my list of awesome."

"More like professional self-promoter," I quipped back.

* * *

Friday, the whole school was energized, and everyone was preoccupied with the build-up to the game. Alumni and parents were in and out bringing snacks and helping put together the giant sign the football team would break through signaling the start of the event. When the last bell rang, we were greeted by the sight of booster Dads already parking their portable grills and smokers at the back of the field, preparing to make the hamburgers and food for the concessions stand.

Jack wasn't at school, but he picked me up pre-game, and we both wore our school-spirit blue and white. I tried to appear calm and sophisticated, like I didn't think anything of his asking me to go with him. But my insides were all mixed up.

I kept it together, and soon we were sitting near the 50-yard line with a good view of the field and the cheerleaders, including Rachel and Renee. Julian joined us, sitting on my left, and though he seemed unusually interested in my welfare, I also noticed him checking out Renee's moves on the field. I told myself I didn't really care what he did. Or what she looked like in her short blue and white skirt. I studied the game and not the confusion swirling inside me.

Brad was almost always on the field focused and in charge of the players. I'd heard talk of his being named All State for the year, and I secretly hoped all that physical exertion would leave him too tired for our little rendezvous on the old beach road. But I hadn't counted on the adrenaline rush we all got when Brad, unable to find an open receiver, was forced to run the ball 50-yards to score the winning touchdown in the final seconds of the game. The fans went wild. Everybody was jumping and screaming, and after post-game interviews and talks, the six of us were headed down to the Gulf, windows down and music blasting.

The old beach road was an abandoned strip of highway cut off from its endpoint by one of the hurricanes, and the dark, sandy-shouldered asphalt was prime real estate for drag racing and all sorts of mischief. Jack and Julian had parked their cars with headlights blazing on Brad's Camaro, and at the moment, they were too caught up in rehashing the game and praising Brad's performance to drive.

"If you'd been in the game tonight, I wouldn't have had to run it." Brad said to Jack. He was still irked that Jack had resisted his pressure to join the team.

"Then you wouldn't be the hero." Jack smiled, patting him on the back.

"Hero," Brad's voice was sarcastic as he stretched his arms back. The light brown knit shirt he wore stretched tight across his muscled chest. "That's how I'll end up getting hurt. I don't need to be a hero. I need a good wide receiver. We'd be winning every game if I had you with me."

"I don't have time for football," Jack breathed, glancing in our direction.

So far our date, or whatever it was, had been strictly platonic. My heart had cooperated somewhat—only once had I been tempted to slide his shaggy bangs off his forehead. What might happen if he tried to kiss me goodnight was anybody's guess, but I was mentally preparing to be strong.

I leaned on the front of the Jeep talking to Rachel while Renee danced to music coming from the car's radio. It was some techno-rap dance song, and before long, I caught the glint of light off a flask in the cluster of guys. That sight made my shoulders tense, but I couldn't stop them. My eyes strained for Julian in the mix. I didn't want him to drive if he'd been drinking. Like he'd listen to me.

"Brad's always so wound up after the games," Rachel said. "And that was such an awesome game; he probably won't even sleep tonight."

"Mmm, lucky you," Renee purred.

Rachel stretched her arms and yawned. "Lucky if we're home before two. I wish they'd hurry up with this."

"I can understand wanting to cheer if it's for your boyfriend like that," I said.

"Yeah," she smiled at me. "Head cheerleader, star of the football team. I guess it's kind of corny."

Her voice was almost sad, so I smiled, hoping to be encouraging. "It's a great memory, and it's just the beginning for you guys."

She gave me a little smile back, and I watched as Renee skipped over to the guys and then twisted a hip around in Julian's direction. He winked and nodded at her. I wrinkled my nose in disapproval.

"You going to share some of that with me?" she said to the threesome. Jack stepped back, walking over to where Rachel and I were sitting.

Renee took the flask from Julian and ran her hand up his thigh as she flicked her hips again. Then she turned and danced back over to where we were sitting. He smiled and flipped at her short cheerleader skirt, and I decided I didn't like Renee Barron as much as I'd previously thought.

"How's Lucy?" I asked as Jack leaned against the Jeep beside me. I needed to distract my mind from worrying how I'd say goodnight to him and caring how Julian would say goodnight to Renee. Both concerns were in direct conflict with my "stronger me" plan.

"Working at the wildlife center has helped," he said, resting his arm on the Jeep behind my shoulders, but still not touching me. "She's found something that interests her."

I wondered if he knew his sister had another interest at the center besides sea grasses and turtles, but I'd let him find that out for himself.

"I was so sorry she had that... trouble." Rachel leaned forward to give him a concerned look.

"Thanks, Rachel. She liked the flowers you sent."

"Want some?" Renee danced up and waved the flask under my nose. I noticed Julian following her. He slipped his arm around her waist from behind and snatched the flask from her hand. She squealed and laughed.

"No, she doesn't. Do you, Banana-face?" His voice held a smirk that set me off for some reason.

I stood and snatched the flask from his hand and quickly took a big gulp faster than anyone could speak. Rachel laughed out loud, but Jack frowned. Julian just looked annoyed and snatched it back, walking away. I had swallowed too much. Tears were welling up in my eyes, but I was too proud to cough, no matter how badly my throat was burning. I tried to swallow again, and I felt Jack's arm go around my waist. He pulled me to the side of the Jeep.

"Something up with you and Julian?" His voice was soft.

"Nobody calls me that." I strangled and finally coughed. Now I remembered why I didn't like whiskey. "I'm sorry. I guess I just snapped. Can we go?"

"I'd like to hang around for a few more minutes. Just to see what they end up doing."

I nodded, feeling warmth from my impulse-slug. It was making me a little woozy. We walked back toward the group, and I saw Julian take a few more hits from the flask before tossing it to Brad, who did the same. Renee was still dancing around, and Rachel was looking at her watch.

"Let's get this show on the road. I'm getting tired," she said.

"Here, first let me show you how it's done," Brad said to Julian as the two climbed through the open windows into the waiting Camaro. Brad cranked the engine and gunned the motor a few times before squealing the tires and shooting off down the road into the darkness. My heart jumped at the loud noise.

"Brad just got that car and now he's going to wreck it." Rachel muttered.

"Doubt it," Jack said. "He knows how to handle a car."

We heard the squeal of tires and could see the headlights pointing back in our direction. Then it shot forward, coming at us fast. I couldn't see what happened. It looked like something small ran into the road. The car swerved and hit the sandy shoulder before jerking back again. Then everything went into slow motion.

I could hear myself screaming as the hood of the Camaro dipped down and the back corner lurched up and over the front. The sound of metal slamming against concrete was louder than a bomb, and I threw my arms over my head as the car flipped twice before rolling to a stop.

My breath was coming in short gasps, and Rachel was screaming now. Jack was no longer at my side. He was running toward the upside-down car. We were all running to it, and then I saw Jack coming back, holding Rachel against him as she fought to get free. Tears were streaming down her face. She kept screaming Brad's name, and I couldn't stop shaking.

With his other hand, Jack touched his phone's face, then I heard him speaking to paramedics. Renee was sitting on the road shaking and holding her knees, rocking back and forth and crying. Pain gripped my sides, and I thought I might be sick. One word kept repeating in my head — *Julian*.

"I've got to go home. I need to go home now," Renee was saying over and over.

"Can you take the Jeep and drive Renee home?" Jack said to me. "I'll wait with Rachel for paramedics."

I nodded, but I was still dazed. I couldn't breathe. I had to get to him.

"Julian," I said. "Is Julian okay?"

"I don't know. I can hear Brad making sounds; they'll be here any minute. Anna, I need you to take Renee home. You guys have been drinking."

I remembered what I'd done, and I couldn't believe I'd been so stupid. I must smell like a distillery. I couldn't stay here.

"Right," I said shaking myself. "I'll take her home, and then, what? South County General?"

"I think that's where they take everyone around here," Jack said.

Rachel still struggled against Jack, but he managed to hold her and was attempting to calm her down as he walked her to Julian's car. I crept away, going slowly to the flipped Camaro. Trembling, I got down on my hands and knees on the damp asphalt and leaned in, my cheek almost to the ground, trying to see anything. It was dark, but I could hear Brad making soft, groaning sounds. My throat knotted as tears stung my eyes.

"Julian?" I said softly. "Oh, god, Julian?"

No answer. I pressed my forehead to the asphalt the tears streaming down my nose. He had to be okay. That little voice I'd pushed down so long was screaming inside me. He couldn't be hurt, he had to survive this.

"Anna, you've got to go now," Jack ordered.

I lifted my head. Renee was freaking out. She had finally stood up and was now pacing. I nodded and rose from the ground, wiping my face with my fingertips as I quickly walked toward her.

"My dad's gonna kill me," she murmured. "I've got to get out of here. I've got to go home now."

I grabbed her arm and dragged her to the Jeep. "Get in." I said, shoving her toward the passenger's side.

I climbed into the driver's seat and slammed the accelerator down, determined to beat EMS to the hospital.

Renee didn't say anything as I drove. She just shook and rocked in her seat. I cranked up the radio and tried not to think of Julian silent, trapped in that car. His art, his plans. I couldn't think of him not being able to pursue his dreams, or worse. Never joking with me again, never touching me...

By the time we reached Renee's house, I was almost in a panic myself. I didn't even kill the engine as she climbed down and shuffled to her door. I pulled out of the driveway before she made it inside and sped back to the road.

The short drive felt like hours, and each red light lasted an eternity. There was so much traffic on the streets in Fairview, it felt like spring break. I wished I knew a back route to the hospital, and by the time I arrived, the boys were already in separate emergency room units with parents called.

Jack and Rachel had the details when I found them. Julian had taken the brunt of the accident. Brad was awake but being held overnight for observation. The doctors were concerned he might have a concussion.

Julian hadn't regained consciousness at all. I thought I would throw up when I heard the words. I had to see him, to be with him. Rachel was calmer, knowing Brad was out of danger, and as the nurses prepared to move him to a private room, I heard his dad blustering down the hallway.

"Where's my boy? Damned sports car. That piece of shit's headed to the junkyard."

Mr. Brennan's way of filling a room made my stomach even more sick, but Jack stepped forward and shook hands with him, giving him the details of the accident. We didn't really know what had caused it; he left out the part involving the flask, although I was sure the doctors could tell alcohol was involved. I had been popping peppermints since we arrived.

The three were slowly making their way down the hall in the direction of Brad's new room when I saw Julian's mom running toward me.

"Anna! Oh, my god! What happened?" Her face was ashen, and I rushed to her. "How is he?"

"I'm not sure, Ms. LaSalle. Jack and Rachel beat me here. I took Renee home."

"Where is he? Who's in charge?"

"Dr. Hayes?" I said unsure. "They have him in one of the ER rooms, but I really don't know more than that. He hasn't regained consciousness yet."

She made a little noise, and her face went completely white. She seemed to be falling, but Jack appeared from behind to catch her.

"I'm sorry," she said, grasping his shoulder and backing into a chair.

"Jack, this is Julian's mom," I said. "Can you tell her what's happening?"

He told her what the doctors had said before I arrived. Julian hadn't regained consciousness, and they were checking him for signs of serious internal injuries. Until he awoke and could answer questions, they were monitoring his condition. I sat next to Ms. LaSalle and put my hand on her arm as she breathed deeply.

"I'll stay with you," I told her. She nodded and rose to find the doctor.

Jack sat in her empty chair and took my hand.

"I'll stay, too," he smiled. "As long as you need me. I know you're worried about your friend."

I nodded and tried to smile back. "Thanks. For all of this. You've been so great, and I know you and Julian aren't especially close."

"Yeah, but Brad's my friend, and I know you care about Julian. Besides, I've gotten a little experience with hospitals lately."

I squeezed his hand and chewed my lip, watching the busy scene. My nerves felt totally frayed. I was worried, and I couldn't stand not knowing what was happening. I wanted to go in and wait at his bedside — to greet his eyes when they opened, to know he was okay. I needed to be closer to him. My chest ached so badly just sitting out here. His mother was at the nurse's station gesturing toward Julian's room, and I turned to Jack.

"It's okay," I said, standing. He stood with me. "I'll call you tomorrow and check in."

His brow lined. "Sure?"

I nodded and stole over to where Ms. LaSalle was. The nurses argued with her, but they took her back to Julian's room. No one noticed as I quietly followed them. Fewer people were scurrying around now, and I waited behind a curtain until everyone went back to their stations.

Inside Julian's room, his mother sat at his bedside, holding his hand. I didn't expect my reaction to the sight of him lying there, pale and lifeless with tubes and wires running toward him. Tears flooded my eyes as pain and fear gripped me hard. My thoughts echoed his mother's prayers.

"Oh, God, please. Don't take him from me." Ms. LaSalle wept. "He's all I have."

She put her head down on his bedside. I inhaled a shaky breath and walked forward slowly. I placed my hand on her arm. She needed someone right now.

"Julian is strong and healthy," I said. "I know he'll pull through. He has to."

She nodded and smiled, sitting up and grabbing a tissue, trying to be strong. "I suppose I should be worrying about how we'll pay for all of this."

I leaned over and hugged her.

"Don't worry about that now. Try not to think about it. Try to focus on him getting better."

She relaxed some and placed her head against my arm, still stroking the top of Julian's hand on the bedside.

"Want to get some coffee or something?" I said. "I'll find you if anything changes."

"I don't know if I should leave him…"

"I'll be here."

She nodded and went to the door, and I was alone with Julian, listening to the beeping sound of the monitors and staring at his closed eyes. I looked at his dark hair and motionless body. Fear tightened my chest, and I said my own silent prayer. I leaned forward and slid my hand under his and held it.

"Oh, Julian. Please be okay," I whispered, leaning forward on the bed. I slid my fingers across the top of his hand, across the little dragonfly, and for a moment, I had the strangest urge to kiss it. But I didn't.

"This is all your fault," I said in my best bantering tone. "You had to show off. Now you'll be lucky if you finish your runner. And I'll lose a night's sleep holding your hand."

Nothing changed, and my face broke. I laid my head on the bedside as the sobs shook my shoulders. The sound of beeps punctuated the background, and the idea that he might never wake up pushed into my brain. I panicked at the thought.

"Oh, Julian. Please. Please wake up." I whispered, my chest painfully tight, eyes damp. "I love you."

My eyes closed at the words I'd never allowed myself to say. For a moment I waited, allowing them to have a place in my mind. Then I stood and paced the small room. I had to get a grip. It hadn't even been four hours since the accident, and I was giving up. I was pouring out my heart to him like it was a deathbed confession, and he could wake up at any moment. For all I knew, he could be awake right now and playing with me. I leaned over his face and looked closely at his eyes. Wishful thinking.

I decided to walk back to the lobby and get a drink of water, because I was clearly going crazy back here alone. I texted Mom as I walked slowly, explaining what had happened in as neutral terms as possible and telling her I planned to spend the night here. I couldn't believe how easily she agreed. I was about to text back when I was distracted by voices speaking in urgent tones in a back corner of the ICU. One was Ms. LaSalle, and for a second I stood in the shadows trying to place the other, male voice. It was so familiar...

"I came as soon as I heard. Is there anything I can do?" I peeked around the corner to see Bill Kyser! He was embracing Julian's mom, and she was holding onto him as if they were more than friends. She rested her head on his chest.

"I'm so glad you're here," she breathed. "I wouldn't have called you, but... It means a lot."

He raised his hand and lightly touched the side of her cheek. It was so intimate, I felt like I must be dreaming. Had I fallen asleep? I had never seen Mr. Kyser so gentle with anyone.

"Try not to worry," he said softly. "I'm sure he'll be okay."

"I can't lose him, Bill. He's all I have."

Ms. LaSalle inhaled sharply as if she were fighting tears again, and Mr. Kyser's arms tightened around her. He kissed her head, and his voice was tender and soothing.

"Stop now. You know that's not true. I know you're scared, but listen to me. Julian is going to be fine."

As if remembering something, she stepped away from him, wiping her tears with her hands and clearing her throat, pushing her hair back and straightening her blouse.

"I was so sorry to hear about Lucy," she said, her tone more formal. "I wanted to let you know I felt terrible about what happened."

He nodded. "She's doing better. And it seems to have ended things."

"I was afraid I'd have to call you about that. I didn't know what to do. Lucy's such a pretty girl, and she's so sweet. So like Meg. I didn't see a way out of it besides…"

"I think that's all over now," he said.

She nodded, and he took her hand, pulling it to his lips. She closed her eyes and looked down. They stood holding hands for a long moment, and then reluctantly it seemed, he released her.

Ms. LaSalle turned her back to him and spoke. "How are you?" she said. "I haven't seen you in a while, but you look… good."

Mr. Kyser's blue eyes were as open as I'd ever seen them. It was almost heartbreaking the way he looked at her, like her voice was a cool drink of water on a burning hot day. I felt embarrassed like I was reading someone's diary, but he cleared his throat.

"The same. Business, the kids. Lucy's always in trouble, but the boys seem to have good heads on their shoulders. Will's a bit ambitious, but Jack never disappoints."

"I saw him tonight. So handsome," she glanced at Mr. Kyser and smiled. "Like you at that age... very much the white knight."

Those words seemed to cause him pain.

"Will he go into medicine?" she asked.

"What?" Mr. Kyser frowned. "Oh, no. Jack's going into business with me."

"Of course," she nodded. "Just, seeing him here reminded me of Dr. Weaver."

Mr. Kyser turned and his eyes landed on me standing behind the curtain. I had been trying to go back to Julian's side, but I was frozen in place by the scene playing out in front of me. He straightened and immediately became the Mr. Kyser I knew.

"I'd better go," he murmured and gestured ever so slightly in my direction.

"What?" Ms. LaSalle seemed stunned, and I felt terrible that I'd stayed. I didn't know what in the world I'd stumbled upon, but I did know these two were historic loners. Yet they clearly knew each other on an intimate level. Then I came along and screwed it all up. I tried to run back to Julian.

"Anna? Is that you?" Ms. LaSalle called me out from the shadows.

"Uh, yes, ma'am. I was coming to get a drink of water. I didn't mean to—"

"It's all right. Mr. Kyser and I are old friends. We both went to high school together, and Bill has known Julian since he was a little boy."

He has?

158

"Anna." Mr. Kyser nodded in my direction. I smiled and nodded back.

"Right," I said. "Well I'm just, you know, looking for the water fountain. I'm sorry."

"Goodnight," Mr. Kyser said. "Goodnight to you both, and Alex, please don't worry about this. I'll take care of it."

Was he talking about the hospital bill?

"I can't let you do that," she protested.

"It's the least I can do." He glanced at me. "Julian took care of Lucy when... well, when she had her accident. Think of it as my way of saying thank-you."

"It's too much." She took his arm and pulled him away from where I was standing. I tried to stop listening and look for the water fountain. *Where was it?*

"Let me take care of this, Lex," he insisted, and I heard Ms. LaSalle protest again.

"You'd better go," she said. "Dr. Hayes is working tonight, and if he sees us together, it might raise questions."

"Travis Hayes? I'd like to see him try and make trouble."

"Please, Bill."

"I'm taking care of this."

"Fine. I just... I don't want it to turn into anything more."

"When have you ever had to worry about that?" His voice was gentle, and I heard movements. I wondered if he would kiss her. I was still looking at the floor, the wall, the ceiling—anything!—when I heard Ms. LaSalle approaching me. I turned and smiled to greet her.

"I'm sorry about that, Anna. I don't have any family left in the area, and Bill and I have known each other a long time," she said. "He just came to check on us."

"There's nothing to apologize for!" I said quickly. "I'm sorry I interrupted your conversation. I really am."

We went back to Julian's room to wait and pray for him to come around. Julian's mom took the recliner, and I sat in the chair beside his bed. My head was so full of all that had happened, I wasn't sure I could be still, and the nurses would be coming in and out all night, monitoring his condition. But I must've fallen asleep because the next thing I knew it was morning, and I could feel a hand on the back of my head. I sat up and it dropped to the mattress. Julian's eyes slowly opened.

I almost burst into tears. "Julian!"

"Heeey, gorgeous," his voice was weak. "I was wondering what I had to do to get you to spend the night with me."

"Oh, Julian!" I pulled up his hand and kissed it. Then I held it to my cheek. "I'm so glad you're awake. I was so afraid..."

"Shh, I'm fine. You think I'd leave here without my angel?"

"Let me get your mom. She'll be so happy you're awake."

"Hey, wait a sec." His hand tightened around mine.

"What? What is it? Does something hurt?"

"I just wanted to thank you for staying. I didn't act right, and I'm sorry. You know I love you, Anna."

I blinked away from his eyes, unable to answer that. I wasn't ready to hear it from him, and I wasn't even sure if he meant it or if it was just the drugs in his system. I decided to treat it as our usual banter.

"Funny way of showing it," I said, pushing his hand gently. "But you didn't do anything. I'm the one sorry. I was being a jerk. It's none of my business what you do with Renee."

160

"That's not what I meant—"

"Let me get your mom," I cut him off as I backed out of the room. "It's not right to leave her waiting. She's been crying and praying all night."

He leaned back and pressed his lips into a smile, letting me go for now.

Chapter 17

Brad was released from the hospital several days before Julian with a clean bill of health. The student body was relieved. There had been vigils all week and prayers for the football star's recovery. Miraculously, he hadn't suffered any serious injuries, and the doctors had ruled out a concussion by Day 2. He could even resume football with the next game.

Julian, on the other hand, hadn't fared as well. In addition to the head injury, he had a fractured wrist and three cracked ribs, which delayed his return to school. I visited him at home after the first week and found him in his garage workshop throwing pieces of metal and cursing. A piece of scrap sailed past me as I entered, and I saw him wince and sit down gasping.

"Hey, what are you doing?" I cried, running to him. "Are you okay?"

"Sorry. The ribs. Feels like knives," he breathed. "And I'm just, I can't do anything."

He slammed another tool on the ground and grimaced. "I can't believe how stupid this is."

"Well, I don't think the doctors would approve of you throwing heavy metal objects around," I smiled smoothing his hair. Then I stopped myself. I shoved my hand in my pocket. "Besides you almost hit me in the head, and I'm trying to be the one person I know not hospitalized."

He smiled and looked up at me. "I was thinking I'd focus on smaller things for now," he said. "This might be the time to make that extra piece of jewelry. You want a ring or something?"

"I thought you needed everything for your portfolio?"

He reached for me. "You can loan it to me when I go for my interview, and I'll bring it back to you. I promise."

"Why don't you make me some earrings or a bracelet or something?"

"I'm making you a ring, now give me your hand."

I smiled and held it out. He pulled me closer, and while he was examining my fingers and comparing them to different sized objects, I looked around the room at his equipment. I hadn't actually noticed it before, but some items looked very expensive. Like the red and black control box for his welding. It had Lincoln stamped on it.

"So do you borrow this equipment from school or what?"

"Huh?" He had stopped measuring and was now simply holding my hand in both of his. "No way. You kidding? They don't let me take anything from school. Too expensive."

"So where did you get all this? I can't believe you bought it all yourself."

"You calling me a thief?" He grinned.

"Well, you did make off with Boze's tattoo gun." I slipped my hand away and walked over to one of the machines.

"Christmas presents, birthdays. I don't know. Mom has a stash somewhere or she's really good at saving. I just say thank you and try to take care of it." He stood and walked over to his table. "Now tell me what you like. Shells? Butterflies?"

"I like everything you make," I said. "Surprise me."

"Good," he smiled. "I was hoping you'd say that."

"So, other than the ribs, how are you feeling?"

"Frustrated. I could've really messed things up that night. I wasn't thinking straight."

"Don't beat yourself up about it. I mean, you've already been hospitalized, and we were all out there blowing off steam. Just... you know, learn from it and move on." I was quiet a moment, thinking back to the accident, what I'd seen. "So did Brad hit something?"

"I think he overcorrected. It happened so fast. I don't really remember."

I remembered. I couldn't forget the terrible sound of metal scraping asphalt and the horrible loud banging of the car going end over end. It made me shudder and feel ill every time I thought about it.

"You don't remember anything?" I said.

"No, and I'm glad because Brad's had trouble sleeping ever since. Post-traumatic stress or something. He called to say he was sorry, but c'mon. It would've been me driving if it wasn't him. I'm not holding a grudge."

I ran my finger down the side of a metal fender. "Rachel said he felt really bad about the whole thing. How he got off without a scratch, and you were pretty beat up."

"Nothing I won't recover from," Julian frowned. "And that's what's pissing me off. I could've died."

"Stop it," I said shaking my head. "I was there, and I don't want to think about that ever again. You scared me to death."

He moved toward me this time and wrapped his good arm around my shoulders, pulling me into an awkward hug, protecting his injured ribs.

"Hey, I'm fine, no worries." He said softly. Then he caught my eyes with his. "So why'd you stay? I mean,

Mom was there, and you knew I was going to be okay. You didn't have to spend the night at the hospital."

I stepped carefully out of his embrace. "I think you are brain damaged. We did not know you were okay, and your poor mom was a wreck. Somebody had to stay with her."

Now that I thought about it, somebody had tried to stay with her and maybe would have if I'd gone home. But my answer wasn't entirely true. I'd stayed because I couldn't leave him. Nothing could have pulled me from his bedside until his eyes opened and I heard his voice, saw that smile again.

"Blaming my mom. You know I came around way before morning." He slid a curl around his finger. "You're very pretty when you sleep."

I turned away and picked up a welder's lens that was sitting on the table. Again, I didn't know how to respond. One little part of me was flying, but the rest of me was still conflicted.

"I was thinking about your mom," I said instead. "Does she ever date anybody?"

"Nah. She said she doesn't have time to train another man."

I laughed, but I wondered if Julian knew about his mom and Mr. Kyser's mysterious connection.

"So like when you go to college, she'll be here by herself?"

"What are you, her new accomplice? She doesn't need your help reminding me of that."

"Be serious. What's the deal? Your mom's so pretty."

"I don't know, Anna. She doesn't date, and as far as I know, she never has. After my dad, I mean."

"Yeah, and so what about that? Do you know your dad? Does he live around here? Maybe she's still in love with him."

He shook his head. "She won't talk about it, and I've always felt bad trying to make her. It's not a good memory for her. And anyway, I don't care who he is. What difference would it make? He obviously doesn't care about me."

I hadn't expected his tone to become sharp, and now I felt bad for prying into his personal business. He was recovering from a serious accident, and I was adding to his stress.

"I'm sorry. It's totally none of my business. I didn't mean to make you feel bad or bring up a bad subject."

"It's okay," he shrugged. "I don't really waste a lot of time worrying about the guy, I guess."

My eyes traveled around the room, and I saw the soldering iron on the table. A few silver nuggets were near it and some sketches. I walked over and looked at them.

"Is this for the ring you keep telling me about?"

He joined me at the table. "Yours? You bet."

"Show me what you've done."

"I'm just planning, but look at this." He picked up the pencil and made a few quick lines and shadings on one of the sketches. On the sheet were three possibilities, and I loved them all.

"Is it a dragonfly?" I asked.

"What better for my angel? And isn't there some lore about dragonflies being angels or something?"

"Oh, Julian. You're always saying that, and it's not true."

He glanced at me, my face close to his shoulder, and dropped the pencil, catching my chin. "Come here," he whispered. Then he pulled my face to his and kissed me firmly on the mouth.

My hands went to his shoulders, frozen between pushing him back and pulling him closer. I inhaled his beachy scent, tasted the salt on his tongue. I'd wanted this for two days, since the wreck, since the idea of losing him first flashed its horrible image across my brain. I'd wanted it since before then, so many times, but I'd always thrown up reasons to distance us. Now I only wanted him closer, I wanted to hold onto him...

But I couldn't. Not yet. Shaking my head, I broke the moment.

"No?" His voice was soft. Pushing him away tore at my insides. He touched my cheek, and our eyes met. "You're still saying no?"

I was nearly overwhelmed by my desire to kiss him again, but I had to face the truth. Jack still lurked in the background of my heart. Some nights I still dreamed of being in Jack's arms, of his lips against mine and running my fingers through his hair. When I awoke, as much as I hated it, as much as it hurt, I wished I could go back to sleep and dream it all again. I couldn't pull Julian into that. He deserved better.

I looked down, and he smiled. "Okay. I was just checking. Again."

I wanted to say the words that were bubbling behind my lips, to tell him how I felt, as horrible and mixed up as it was, but I bit them back. Shut that little voice.

"I'd better go. I just stopped by to see if you were feeling better. I didn't mean to stay."

"Yeah," he breathed, limping back to his art table. "See you at school."

I nodded and walked away, hoping it wasn't obvious that I was fighting the urge to run. He'd never understand why. I wasn't sure I did.

* * *

Mom was watching a documentary on public television when I arrived home that night, so I grabbed a sandwich and ran upstairs, pulling out my phone.

My best friend called a muffled hello. "What are you eating?" I asked.

"Bugles," Gabi crunched, and I knew she had a pointy chip stuck on all five of her fingertips—her favorite way to eat them. "You only call me when there's a problem. So go."

I let out a small laugh and rested my forehead on my palm, unexpected tears filling my eyes. "Julian and Brad were in a wreck and—"

"Stop now!" Gabi cried. "Tell me my Julian is okay!"

"You're doing it again," I sighed. "He was never *your* Julian—"

"Shut up and tell me he's okay. His face is undamaged, and… all the rest of him."

"He's fine, but that's the problem." I felt nervous saying it out loud. "I kissed him."

"Who?"

"Julian."

"What!" Gabi cried again. "I hate you, and I hope you get trapped under something heavy." She crunched loudly in my ear.

"Gabi! Stop! I wasn't trying to kiss him. I was trying to see if he was okay. Like always. But then he kissed me. And I was right there kissing him back."

"Yeah, you were! Julian's smokin' hot, and now you're friends with benefits."

"It's not like that."

"Yet." *Crunch.* "I'm having a hard time seeing the problem here."

"Jack and I went to the game together Friday."

"Jack?" Her voice was a shriek. "I thought he was history!"

"So did I." I fell back on the bed groaning loudly. "I don't know what he wants. He hurts me, and we aren't even together. He pushes me away, and when he pulls me back, I run to him."

"Do you really like him?"

"I don't know." My emotions were in shambles, and even saying it seemed wrong. "I still dream about Jack, but inside me wants to be with Julian. How do I even cope with that? It's insane."

"What else do you have going on? How's life in the news business?"

"I love it, and Nancy has me working on this huge project that's going to look amazing on my résumé."

"So focus on that."

I inhaled deeply and closed my eyes. "They keep sneaking up on me. These moments, stealing my breath. And I think I should follow my instincts, but I keep messing up. I keep making the wrong choice."

"You're definitely having an interesting year."

"Rachel says it's because you left. She said I hid behind you."

"Hmm," I heard her crunch. "Maybe. But I don't know. Moving's hard, breaking into a new place and all. You were just figuring it out."

"I didn't know I was doing that," I said quietly, my eyes growing warm.

She stopped crunching, and her voice grew serious. "Okay, Banana-face. Enough. We can solve this. First, what do you want? Maybe if you defined your goals, you'd make the right choice."

"I don't know," I said, trying to feel stronger. "I planned all this out before school started. I was going to beef up my résumé, make sure I had everything with the best journalism schools. Then Dad suggested trying for a scholarship."

"That's all good."

"I want to keep writing," I sighed. "Otherwise, I just want to be happy."

"So does everybody. Get more specific. What would make you happy?"

My brain felt empty and tired, and thinking about it frustrated me. "I don't know."

A loud exhale met my ear. "Let's take a different approach. What do you not want? Define that, and maybe it'll lead you to what you do."

"It's a good idea," I said, thinking.

"That's your assignment," Gabi said, resuming her crunch.

"Hey, thanks."

"Just doing my job."

"'night, Gab."

"'night."

I hung up the phone, wishing for the millionth time she was still here. Closing my eyes, I thought of her advice. What I didn't want...

I didn't want to be an after-thought. I wanted to be the first thought. I didn't want to be cast aside or with someone who was only interested when I was no longer available.

I wanted to have value. I did have value.

My brain flooded with images of what that meant. Of me being the reason for someone to keep trying; of them being the reason for me.

It was working. I felt calmer, stronger. I began to understand what it meant. What I wanted and what I needed to do. I was going to follow my dreams, and I was going to find my way to the right person. It would take a little time, I knew it would take more work, but my confidence was growing. I smiled as I believed it would happen. I was going to make it through this.

Chapter 18

Nancy was in the back room of the archives digging in a huge box of pictures when I arrived at the newspaper office.

"We really should start scanning these," she muttered. "Anna, is your mom still at the association office or is she working on the fundraiser?"

She handed me a picture of some young people at what looked like Scoops twenty years ago. The trees were thinner, and I loved the vintage outfits they were wearing.

"I don't know, what's this?" I asked.

"I found these old images of Fairview kids. I think I've got one in here of Alex LaSalle, and I need a photographer to get in the old Magnolia Hotel and take pictures of her paintings if they're still hanging. Could your mom let somebody in over there?"

"Ms. LaSalle was an artist?"

"Painter," Nancy said. "Considered a real comer for a while. She moved back here from Atlanta to help Bill Kyser with some of his developments. I'm not sure what happened, but after a couple of years, she suddenly retired. Didn't want any publicity, tried to erase all memory of her painting career. I thought I'd give her a call and see if she's softened up some now that her kid's doing so well. That was part of the reason we picked up your feature. Locals will remember her and put the two together."

My head was spinning. Julian had never told me his mom was a painter. *Moved back to help Bill Kyser?*

I thought about that night at the hospital and grabbed the picture again, studying the faces leaning against a car near the old drive-through. Even in black and white I recognized her fair skin and beautiful bone structure framed with long, dark-brown hair. She was exactly the same. And standing right next to her was a face that could've been Jack's but with light brown hair.

"Who's that?" I knew the answer, but I wanted to be sure. He had the same killer smile that made me forget everything logical.

"Oh, that's it," she laughed. "That's Alex with Bill and Meg Kyser. Look how young and handsome he was. Meg was so pretty... Too bad about all that."

I grabbed the picture back and saw now that his arm was around what could've been Lucy, same long blonde hair, looking at his face with an enraptured smile. I knew that feeling.

"That's his wife that died?" I asked.

"Yeah. Sad story. Local girl dies young, leaves behind three babies and a grieving husband."

I almost couldn't breathe. "What happened exactly?"

"Car crash. I'm sure we have the write-up in here somewhere. Those guys are a little older than me, but I remember they were all friends. He and Meg got married when I was in middle school. Big local event. I don't remember the exact year, but I'd graduated and moved away when the accident happened."

"But why would Ms. LaSalle just retire from art like that?"

"I don't know," Nancy said, standing up and straightening her blouse, smoothing her hair back. "I'm planning to see what I can find out if she'll talk to me. Will you call your mom?"

"It's better if I walk over. She doesn't always hear the phone ring."

I walked back to the front office to grab my coat with the old images in my head. Ms. LaSalle's face was as serious then as it was now, and I was amazed at how much Jack looked like his dad—just like she'd said at the hospital.

But the way they were all standing in the picture, I didn't see any signs of romance. Not then, at least. Mr. Kyser's arm was around his wife's shoulders, and she was holding his waist. It was just friends leaning against an old car in front of what looked like a very different version of our town.

Heading to the door, I froze in the hallway. The steel grey Jeep was parked out front, and leaning against it, looking at his phone was Jack. My heart beat harder, but I clenched my teeth against it. Turning to the wall and watching him, I tried to decide what to do.

Last night I'd made my goals, and if I were going to be valued, he didn't have the best track record. But seeing him there, leaning against the jeep, dressed in jeans and a dark tee with a blazer on top, it felt so silly to make goals and hold myself to them when that was waiting for me. All I wanted was to go to him. I wanted to smooth the messy bangs from his eyes. I wanted him to kiss me.

"Ugh," I quietly growled, banging my forehead lightly against the wall. "What is wrong with me?"

I took a deep breath, put on a confident face, and went through the glass doors. "What are you doing here?"

That smile crossed his lips, and I hated the way my body responded to him. It wasn't fair. "Hey," he stepped forward and kissed my cheek. He smelled like the beach, and images of him on the water filled my mind. Damn images.

I smiled back, heart pounding. My mouth actually watered. "Did you have a news event to report?"

He laughed. "No. I had to come up to the office for Dad, and I thought you might like to get some dinner with me."

I held my expression steady. He was doing it again—asking me out when he'd said we weren't together. "Tonight?"

"Sure—you already have a date?" His confident grin said he knew I didn't. Of course I didn't.

"Is that what it is? A date?"

"Friends go to dinner all the time. I was planning to drive over to Jesse's. Let me treat you."

That ritzy little café tucked away on the banks of the Magnolia River was a place I'd only heard stories about. Some kids could afford to go there before prom, but for the most part, it had an exclusively older clientele.

"You want to take me to Jesse's."

"Would you rather grab a burger?"

I shook my head with a little laugh. "I would love to go with you to Jesse's. Let me finish here. I've got to tell mom to call Nancy, and I wish I had time to change…"

The khaki skirt and light-blue sweater I'd pulled on this morning didn't feel fancy enough. I looked down at my black boots and wished I had more than a cropped denim jacket to go over it.

"You look great. I'll pick you up in a half hour." He smiled in that way that warmed my whole body, and I knew this was a mistake. But I was making it.

I'd deal with my shredded insides later.

* * *

Jesse's sat on a tree-lined stretch of river that extended down to Coyote Bay and then out to the Gulf of Mexico. Our table was on the patio and twinkle lights lined the tin roof of the intentionally rustic-looking establishment. It wasn't a crowded night, and a collection of tea lights in the center of the table made the setting romantic and beautiful.

"This is really nice," I said.

"I was just thinking this is our first date," he said, putting his napkin in his lap.

"And we're not even together anymore." I had to get that part out on the table.

His blue eyes studied mine. "Sometimes it can be interesting to do things backwards."

I had no idea what that meant, but I didn't care. I'd be damned if I wasn't going to enjoy this dinner. I'd earned it.

"We went sailing a few times," I said. "Those can count as dates. How's *Slip Away*?"

"Lonely. Maybe you need another lesson after all."

What was he doing? I studied his face in the yellow glow, and I couldn't decide what I saw there. It was like regret, but not quite. More like control. "I'm booked this weekend. Mom's association has set up a giant hay maze fundraiser."

A smile broke his cheeks. "Sounds fun. Is it haunted?"

"Of course. Why would anyone have a hay maze the last weekend in October, and it not be haunted? A group's going Saturday night. Want to tag along?"

"Sure. Should I to pick you up?"

I thought about my plans to catch a ride with Mom, but I didn't mind going later. "Sure," I said with a smile, thinking about that night, this night. We were just being friends... right?

"So now that you have your own English class," I said. "What do they have you reading? Anything good?"

"I have to read *Sense and Sensibility*. Most teachers assign *Pride and Prejudice*, but my reaction is the same. Wordy chick lit."

"Terrible response!" I cried. "If that's all it is, then why would it have survived this long?"

"Most teachers are chicks."

"Jack!" I pushed his hand. "I think it's an amazing study of both the helplessness of the sisters at that time in society and the complexity of their different personalities. I mean, look at Marianne, all passion and drama, almost dying when Willoughby rejects her. Compared to Elinor who's so quiet and reserved, but fiercely loyal and probably stronger in her devotion even without the outward display."

Jack's blue eyes watched me in the candlelight, and I felt a self-conscious tingle in my stomach. "I guess I'm boring you to death."

"I like hearing what you think." The grin on his lips was killing me. "When you talk about these books we're reading, I actually start to care about them. You should be a teacher."

"Thanks," I rolled my eyes and adjusted my napkin. "That's very sexy."

"Yes. The sexy librarian."

My eyes flickered back to his. "That's a myth. I have never seen a sexy librarian."

"I've seen a few."

Then I laughed. "Why are you checking out librarians?"

"Just looking around," he said. "You might be one."

"Right." What the hell? *Was Jack saying I was sexy?* Suddenly this felt a lot more than friendly.

The waiter appeared and Jack ordered smoked duck and gouda for starters then the Delmonico ribeye with smashed potatoes. I grinned. "Meat and potatoes?"

"It's the best. Should I order the same for you?"

"Sure, but let me try these gouda grits."

He handed our menus to the waiter with a wink. "Two of the same, but grits for the transplant."

An acoustic trio was playing classic rock songs at the far end of the patio, and one couple had risen to dance. Jack stood and held out his hand. I'd never danced in a fancy restaurant, but it was so empty, I figured what the hell. He pulled me close against his firm chest, and we swayed to the tune as I tried not to melt in his arms. I was so going to regret this, and I wasn't changing a thing.

Images of my palms on his bare chest, us on the beach, in his bedroom, I wanted so much more than "just friends." I wanted to pull his face down and kiss him. But I wouldn't. I could at least preserve my pride, even if I was barely breathing.

The song ended and we strolled back to the table holding hands. Our food was waiting for us, but I didn't feel like eating. The steaks were perfectly cooked, slightly pink in the middle, but I could only manage a few bites. My stomach was tight, and while part of me wanted to let loose and indulge, the other part was on edge, wondering what was coming.

Jack studied my plate. "Don't like it?"

"It's delicious. I'm just tired all of a sudden. Long day, I guess."

He smiled. "We can take off."

I waited while he settled the bill, and soon we were back in the Jeep headed southeast toward home. The top was off, but the crisp fall air didn't wreak as much havoc with my curls as in the summertime. I was starting to relax until we turned toward the beach road instead of town. I looked over at him.

His eyes were on the road. "Want to look at the water?"

"Sure," I said, studying his profile, the wind pushing his hair around his face.

He parked in the same lot as the first time we came here after that first dance. With the engine off, the sound of the breakers crashing and the hiss of the surf were loud and close. The salty ocean-smell was strong.

"I'm going to miss this," he said under his breath, sliding his hands from the wheel to his lap. "Sometimes at night, I leave all the windows open so I can hear it."

I nodded. "It always helps me relax."

His eyes moved to me, and he held out his hand. I put mine in it, and he pulled gently. For a half-second, I hesitated. Then I crossed the space between us, letting him pull me onto his lap facing him in a straddle. His warm hands found the skin under my sweater and his mouth was on my neck just as fast. My whole body was instantly burning, and I tried to calm my flying heart. But it was pointless. I was gone.

"Do friends make out?" I managed to say, eyes closed.

"Good friends," he said against my skin before slipping a hand behind my neck and pulling my mouth to his.

The hand on my back traveled higher, loosening my bra, and I slid my fingers into his hair as he caressed me. I was moving, kissing him deeply, my heart pounding as the pressure built low in my stomach. The feelings were so intense, so good, I didn't care what was coming. I didn't care if I cried tomorrow or all week. I broke away to gasp for air, and his hands moved to my hair, pulling my ear to his mouth.

"Let me in," he whispered, then kissed me. I frowned, not sure I understood. My confusion disappeared when his hands went under my skirt, adjusting my position as he found the line of my panties.

My stomach clenched as I placed my hands on his shoulders. "Here?" I whispered, my forehead against his. I kissed the tip of his nose. "Can't we go somewhere else?"

He kissed my jaw, burning a trail to my cheek and covering my mouth again. He slid me forward against him, teasing me, before he pulled back. "What's wrong?"

I shook my head. "I just… I kind of wanted my first time to be a little more… special."

Everything stopped.

Jack leaned his head back against the head rest and closed his eyes. I watched his lips form a straight line as he moved his hands to my waist on top of my sweater, exhaling slowly.

"What?" My voice sounded small to me.

His eyes opened, blue crashing into hazel. "I'm sorry. I forget how young you are," he said. "I'll take you home."

"Home?" I repeated, confused. "That's it?"

He didn't answer, and I climbed off his lap and moved across the Jeep, back to my side. My heart thudded as shame filled my chest. Anger followed close behind. I shouldn't be ashamed, and I wasn't that young. Pulling my knees up, I looked out the window as he turned the key. I didn't speak as he drove us the short distance to my house.

The moment the vehicle stopped moving, I jumped out and ran to my door. I quickly went inside and slammed it, turning the lock. All those good ideas, those goals I'd spent so much time working on were so quickly forgotten. I ran up the stairs to my bathroom and turned the water on full-blast before sliding to the floor. With my back against the cabinet, I kicked my leg out in front of me. I pounded my fists against the rug as the angry tears fell.

He couldn't make me feel this way if I didn't let him. That's what they always said, right? Pain twisted in my chest, and I cried harder, hugging my knees to my stomach.

Why couldn't I believe it? Why did I go running every time he crooked his finger my way only to be tossed aside again because I was too young or required too much effort or he didn't have time. Was that me? Was I that weak?

Oh, god. Tears drenched my cheeks, and I didn't even try to stop them. But after a few moments, I helped myself up, avoiding my reflection in the mirror. I bent over and splashed cool water on my face, taking a rag and soaking it. Then I crossed the hall and crawled into bed.

Chapter 19

The strange thing about fall along the Gulf Coast was the flowers. Everywhere you looked impatiens and begonias were sporting happy blossoms. It was like spring all over again. Crepe myrtle trees were bursting with lavender, white, and all shades of pink. Encore azaleas were ablaze with color, and even the ubiquitous palms were showing the white blossoms at their hearts. And it was all shoved right up next to red, orange, and yellow nylon-leaf garlands and plastic jack-o-lanterns — things not found naturally in this area.

After three years here, I still missed fall in the Midwest. I missed it being frosty every morning by now and the cool sweater weather that made scary movies so much more fun to watch. I missed hot cider at apple orchards and low humidity. The only problem was that back home sweater weather soon turned into heavy coat weather, and it lasted months longer than everyone wished it would. And we never had blazing azaleas in the Midwest or miles of turquoise waters crashing on sugar-white sands.

The last two days had felt like two years with me trying not to think about Jack, trying to suppress my blazing cheeks the few times I did. He sent a few texts that remained unread, and his one call was sent to voicemail. I didn't want to read an apology if that was what he was offering, and I couldn't hear his voice. If he was saying anything else, it would only make it worse.

My thoughts were miles away when I heard the friendly voice calling my name. Only one voice was able to cut through it all. One person could make me forget that pain like a warm massage to the heart. I looked up and Julian was crossing the parking lot in the direction of my car. Black trousers, white oxford, shaggy dark head, as usual. Only today his left sleeve was rolled to the elbow above his cast.

"Wait up—I have something to show you," he called.

He appeared very much back to normal, cute as ever, and pulling a white bundle from his back pocket.

"Hey," I said as he got closer. "You're looking much better."

"Ribs have eased up a lot," he smiled and my shoulders relaxed. I leaned against the car, and he stood in front of me unrolling the paper.

I watched his progress curiously. "What is it?"

"This." He held it open, and I almost squealed. It was my ring! I forgot everything as my book bag slid to the ground

"Oh, look at it!" I cried softly. "It's so beautiful!"

It was shining silver with a tiny, rainbow-sparkling dragonfly across the center. I reached forward to touch it carefully.

"I wanted it to fit you," he watched my face as I studied it.

I lifted the delicate piece. "How did you make it sparkle?"

"Mom gave me a few crystal beads, and I ground them down and mixed them with the silver. I was just experimenting, but it paid off, I think."

My eyes went to his. "I love it."

He took my hand and slipped his unique creation on my right middle finger, seeming very pleased. A lump was in my throat.

"There you go," he said, still holding my hand.

"But don't you need it to show? Maybe you could just dedicate it to me like a book or something."

"I told you, I'll borrow it when I go for my interview," he said. "But it's yours. I want you to keep it."

I couldn't stop looking at my hand, tilting it in the light and watching the sparkles. Julian grinned watching me.

"I'm supposed to be at the paper office. Otherwise," I hesitated. "I don't know."

"Are you coming to the hay maze with everybody tomorrow?"

"Yeah!" I looked up at his face. His eyes flickered to my mouth and then up again.

"Go with me?"

Just then I remembered—and I knew why Jack had probably called me. I looked down, that weight back in my stomach. "I invited Jack to come along. I think he's picking me up."

Julian poked his lips out and nodded. "I get it."

"It's not like—"

"No worries. I'll see you there." He touched my chin with his finger. "Later. Oh, and have fun at the paper, cubby."

"Thanks, Julian." I watched him go, releasing the breath I didn't realize I was holding. This tension was killing me. I needed to check my phone.

* * *

When I got home that night, Mom was in the kitchen stirring a pot of what looked like yellow soup. An oval baking dish sat on the counter, and inside were layers of vanilla wafers and bananas.

"What are you doing?" I asked.

"I'm trying to make a banana pudding," she frowned. "Nana sent me the recipe."

"Banana pudding? That's new. What's it for?"

"We're helping with the hay maze fundraiser, and they want to do a dessert auction. You get the release I sent over?"

"You sent that? Why didn't you tell me?"

"I didn't want to bias your cute little newsy nose," Mom grinned. "Did you send it on?"

"I sure did. And I've got a group of friends going tomorrow for the thriller maze."

"It's going to be a hoot," she chuckled. "Rain Hawkins is getting a bunch of the coaches together. They've got a chainless chainsaw, fake blood. I think the Catman is supposed to make an appearance."

"Catman?" I frowned.

"Half-man, half-wildcat. Local legend."

"Hey, speaking of that, how old were you when Nana and Pop-pop moved to Indiana?"

"Huh? Oh, I was just finishing elementary school, I guess. Why?"

"We were digging through the archives at work. Nancy's working on the bicentennial insert, and she found some old pictures of Ms. LaSalle when she was a senior in high school."

"No kidding," Mom said, thinking. "We've got some of her old paintings in the hotel, you know. She should send a photographer over."

"Funny you said that. That's exactly what she wants to do. I'm supposed to find out when would be a good time."

"Any time. Tell her to call me, and we'll set something up."

"Did you know any of those guys before you left?"

"Alex LaSalle? I knew *of* her. There never have been that many full-time residents here. But we were all kids when I left."

"Did you know Jack's dad?"

"I doubt it," she said. "What's the sudden interest?"

"Nothing. I was just wondering." I poked her in the side. "Remember to answer the phone."

I thought about Mr. Kyser and Ms. LaSalle at the hospital. I wished I could remember what all they'd said to each other. They'd said they were just old friends, but it was obvious they had more of a connection. What did it mean? I was dying of curiosity, and it seemed like a harmless way to get my mind off boy troubles. Of course, I had no intention of ever doing anything with the information or telling anyone. I was simply following Gabi's advice and focusing on work. Doing a little off the record snooping—just for me.

Chapter 20

The thriller hay maze was even bigger than the advertisement had made it sound. Giant speakers blasted spooky noises and eerie music across the grounds, and the place was jammed with groups of teenagers and families with younger kids. Twilight, the crisp air, and screams erupting every few moments from inside the maze created the perfect late-fall adrenaline rush.

Jack didn't say a word about our previous date night or how it had ended when he picked me up, and I wasn't going there. Every time I thought of his expression, how he'd shut down and shut me out, my stomach twisted with shame, which I also knew was stupid.

The upside was these feelings drowned out my frustrating desire for him. I'd returned his text simply verifying what time he could pick me up, and the radio precluded any conversation on the short drive to the pasture off the old county road. I was back to our previous agreement. We were only friends. Nothing more.

We arrived just in time to see Rachel and Brad, wearing orange and black fleece jackets and scarves. They walked over to meet us, and further in I saw Julian looking over the silent auction table. He was dressed in jeans and a dark blue shirt under a brown tweed blazer. His dark hair was tossed to the side, and a small smile touched my lips until I saw he was holding hands with Renee. Then I frowned. I hadn't realized he'd go back to her after we'd talked. Not that I had any right to be mad.

She was dressed in a tight sweater and jeans, and she whispered something in his ear. He smiled and walked away. Then she waved to Rachel, who grabbed my arm and pulled me over to the silent auction area. Each item had a little card beside it to hold the handwritten bids, and I saw a small metal figure that looked like a miniature version of Julian's runner. My finger lightly touched the band of the dragonfly ring hidden under my glove. So far I hadn't taken it off except to bathe and wash my face.

"Hey, Rach! I'm *so* glad you guys are here," Renee said. "We can go through the maze together. It's supposed to be really scary."

"Chicken?" Rachel laughed. "Who set it all up?"

"Mr. Hawkins donated the land, and he got some of the guys from the ranch to help."

Rain Hawkins was one of the few farmers left in South County, and one of Renee's relatives owned a horse ranch in Midlind.

"Is that one of Julian's sculptures?" I asked pointing to the small runner.

"Yeah, I put that together to help out," Julian said, handing a bag of popcorn to Renee.

"Oh, hey," I said, trying to be casual. "I like it."

"Make a bid," he grinned. "I know I've spoiled you, but it's for a good cause."

"Spoiled me?" I frowned. "What..."

"You like something, I make it for you." He smiled, and I looked down again quickly.

"Oh, right," I said.

"What did Julian make for you?" Renee asked.

I noticed Jack and Brad walking toward us. "Looks like we're ready to start," I said, ignoring her.

"One of those Helen Freed pieces." Julian said taking Renee's hand and pulling her toward the entrance. "Who's ready to get lost?

"Didn't somebody see the Catman sneaking around this field?" Brad teased.

"Shut up, Brad." Renee put a handful of popcorn into her mouth.

"Somebody's about to be screaming," Brad sang out.

We handed over our tickets and started into the maze. Renee and Rachel were giggling nervously as we walked, waiting for something to happen. Jack held out his arm to me, and I took it, not minding a little temporary protection, regardless of the source.

It was cooler inside the maze, and the height of the walls made it darker as well. Huge spotlights lit certain portions of the grid, but some corners were almost completely dark. Those were the tense spots, where you could feel the actors lurking, waiting to scare you. It was all in good fun, but I was glad we were going through it as a group.

We rounded the first corner, and from the shadows, I felt the swish of air as something ran toward us from behind. Rachel screamed as a fur-clad figure snarled at her. We scattered in six different directions, screaming and laughing. It was terrifying, and I couldn't stop giggling. I ran as hard as I could from our grisly pursuer, thinking someone was with me, but after several turns, I stopped running and looked around. I was alone. *Great.*

I walked slowly through the dim-lit stacks, straining my ears for familiar voices. I thought I heard Rachel off to my right, and I followed the sound. But as I rounded the corner, it was a shadowy dead end. I doubled back and listened again. It sounded like they were just on the other side of the hay wall, and I started running straight ahead. My heart was thudding when the passage opened. I could go right or left. I waited and listened, and once again, I felt the swish of air as a figure came up behind me. I spun around ready to scream, but it was only Julian.

"Hey," he said low in my hair, as his hands found my sides.

"Julian!" I laughed, hugging him in relief. He smiled and pulled me into a shadowy corner. "I hate being alone in these things, and I thought you were—"

He leaned in and cut me off with a kiss. My heart had been racing from the fright and the running, but now it was flying for a different reason. Instinctively, I pulled him closer, not wanting to let him go, and he held me tighter in response.

This time his kiss was not a question, it was a demand, and the part of me I'd been pushing down for weeks came rushing up to meet him. My arms were around his neck, and I slipped my fingers into his hair. I felt his lips curve into a smile against mine, and our mouths opened, tongues touched, and electricity raced to my toes. It was hot and breathtaking, and everything I'd expected returning Julian's kiss to be like. His uncasted arm circled my waist, holding me strong against his body, then he lifted his head to look into my eyes.

We were both breathing fast. Neither of us spoke, we only smiled, a little amazed and unable to look away. He leaned forward to kiss me again, and once more I kissed him back, open-mouthed and eager. Hungry. I felt confident and strong, and I didn't want to stop ever. He held me back against the scratchy hay wall, and my hands moved from his shirt to his shoulders and then his neck. I wanted to touch his skin. I wanted to pull him closer. I wanted to feel his skin against mine.

His lips moved to my jaw then my chin, and without thinking, I murmured his name. I dropped my face against his neck, inhaling deeply the faint scent of his cologne mixed with the straw all around us. We were swirling in a dizzying wave of adrenaline until I heard voices coming toward us.

As if waking from the most amazing dream, I opened my eyes and reluctantly stepped away, out of Julian's arms.

"I think I heard them over here!" Renee ran up and stopped short, the laughing others close behind her.

I turned away and tried to pick the hay fragments out of my hair. There was no denying what we'd just done, and I didn't know what to say. Going after another person's date wasn't cool, and it wasn't the reputation I was after, even if it was for Julian.

"Hey, Renee." Julian said, clearing his throat.

"What's up, Date? You know, you really should try a different shade of lipstick with your complexion." Her tone was sarcastic.

"I was considering a Goth phase. You say no?" Julian wiped his mouth. Jack appeared with Rachel and Brad close behind.

"Do what you want, Julian. You always do." Renee walked back toward Rachel, who was staring at me.

"Anna, you okay?" Jack came over and took my arm, turning me around. I looked up at him, trying to smile, but I only succeeded in looking sheepish. He hadn't given me any reason to guard his feelings, but still. This wasn't who I wanted to be.

"I... I guess I ran the wrong way," I said quietly. "Julian found me."

Jack frowned. "Your lipstick's smudged."

I couldn't speak.

His lips formed that line again. "C'mon. I know the way out."

He took my hand and led me away from the group. I could hear our friends' low voices as we made our way through the remainder of the maze and away from them. Jack stayed ahead of me, walking with controlled determination. I could tell he was angry, which made me angry, but I followed him past group after group of screaming teenagers being chased by costumed adults. When we reached the exit, he kept walking in the direction of the parking lot.

"Are we leaving?" I asked.

He didn't answer as I followed him to the Jeep.

"I'm headed back," he said. "It's your choice — you can catch a ride with those guys if you want to stay."

"I'm ready to go," I said. Hanging out with a pissed-off Renee was the only thing I could imagine worse than riding home with Jack right now.

Much like the drive over, we rode the whole way back in silence with only the radio playing. Jack looked straight ahead at the road, and I looked out the window at the passing trees. When we got to my house, he stopped and walked around to help me out.

"Thanks for the ride," I said, but he held my arm. My eyes went to his, and I saw a hint of anger simmering there.

"So what was that? Payback?"

"No!" I hated the defensive sound in my voice. "As if you have any right to be mad."

He surprised me with a laugh. "You're right. I have no right. Other than you were there with me tonight."

"As friends," I said. "Which was your decision."

His lips tightened. "Friends. That's right. No matter what happened two days ago."

"Two days ago you reminded me how little you care. I guess I learned sensitivity from watching you." I jerked my arm away as I said it.

"Wrong. Two days ago you didn't give me a chance to explain. And I never went after someone else when I was with you."

"So I'm the bad guy?" I could feel my eyes flashing. I hadn't wanted to fight with him, but I was so happy to clear the air. "Explain please. Tell me how you can go from one hundred percent into me to zero in the space of two words."

"It wasn't that. I was into it, but if I'd gone there, been your first... I won't do that to you. It's exactly why I'm holding back now."

"You're holding back now?" I repeated, disbelief clear in my voice.

He made a move like he might pull me into his arms, but I quickly took a step back.

"No. That's over," I said. "I can't do the casual hook up anymore." But even as I said the words, my trembling insides told me I'd have to work overtime to make them true. I was ashamed to admit how weak I still was when it came to him, how much my body still wanted him to finish what he kept starting in me.

"Thanks for taking me tonight," I continued, not meeting his eyes. "But I need a break."

I could see words forming on his lips, but he didn't answer me. Instead he climbed back into the Jeep and drove away.

I stood several minutes staring after him into the darkness, still trembling with the adrenaline pulsing through my body. I couldn't tell if I was happy or miserable. I'd just sent Jack away. And it was very possible I'd never see him again. A scary sense of loss clutched at my chest, and I turned slowly to my empty house.

Pain forced my shoulders to bend as I exhaled, but I had to be okay with this. Sure, I had chased after the excitement and the sexiness of him. But I had to believe I could mean more to someone than stolen kisses and casual hook ups, always stopping short of anything that required commitment or something more. I had to believe I had value apart from that.

I went upstairs and curled into a ball on my bed, closing my eyes and sliding my thumb back and forth across the band of my dragonfly ring. I didn't cry. I didn't want to cry. I simply lay there trying to understand what I was feeling and what I really wanted.

Chapter 21

Short weeks were all that stood between me and the end of the semester, when I knew Jack would be gone for good. I decided I didn't care. After the Halloween incident, I'd resolved to focus only on my work and on college and not my inability to manage any sort of successful love life. I'd sent Jack away, I'd told Julian I needed time. Now I was going to give myself that time.

That was the plan anyway, but of course, I could never plan for Julian.

He was waiting for me, leaning against Mom's car in the student lot. "Hey, Anna," he said, pushing his dark bangs back.

"Your cast is off," I said, hugging my books to my chest.

He held out his hand, flexing his fingers. "Yeah. Just got it off. I'm working on getting the strength back."

I remembered the night of the birthday party when he'd carried me to the T-bird after I'd fallen—how worried he'd been, how protective. His little dragonfly tattoo was uncovered now, and it was the first time I could see it exactly matched my ring.

"Did you need something from me?" I asked, hating this tension I felt when I was around him now. I wanted things to be easy between us again.

"I should've done this before now." He exhaled, looking down.

"Done what?"

"I'm sorry," he said. "I mean... I'm not sorry it happened. But I'm sorry if you're mad. Or if I hurt you."

"Are you talking about at the maze?"

Blue eyes rose to mine, and my heart did its usual Julian-pull. "Yeah, I guess I went too far that night."

"It wasn't completely your fault. I mean, I didn't exactly fight you."

"I remember." The little grin teasing at the corners of his mouth made me hug my books tighter. Focus.

"I've got to get to the paper office," I said.

He straightened up, moving away from the car. "Sure. I just wanted to tell you that."

I nodded and dug my keys out of my bag. But I stopped before opening the door. "I'm not mad or hurt," I said. "We were all excited, and it was dark. And confusing."

"Were you confused?" He studied my face, and I could feel it turning red.

"No," I said quietly. "But I am now. What I really want is a break. School, going to work, that's all."

"Okay," he nodded. "I'm not pushing you. And I'm not going anywhere. You know, when you feel less confused."

I started to get in the car, but I stopped. "Why?"

His brow creased, but the tiny smile still teased at his lips. "Did you just ask me why?" Then he caught one of my curls. "Are you kidding? Have you seen how cute you are?"

"C'mon, Julian." I shoved the curl behind my ear. "I'm being serious."

He shrugged. "Because you're my angel. You put me on the map. You always believe in me."

"I didn't do anything. You've done it all, and it was just a matter of time before everybody saw it."

He laughed. "See? That's what I'm talking about. Oh, and you're great at math."

I exhaled a laugh then, too. "Yes. So great, you failed the course."

"I might've passed."

My jaw dropped. I couldn't believe it. "Are you saying... Did you fail on purpose? Julian, why?"

He touched my nose. "Why do you think? And then you went and quit on me."

"That's why you were mad," I said, remembering his odd reaction our first day back. "And now you have to take it again."

"Now I'm aceing it, and it's my last math."

I shook my head. "I've got to get to work."

"Later, Sunshine."

* * *

Our project at the paper office made focusing on work almost fun. Nancy had me tracking down anything I could find about Ms. LaSalle for her proposed feature, and I was free to dig through the archives and secretly snoop at will. But I ran into a major road-block. It seemed that even though Julian's mom was a popular local artist, news about her was nonexistent. Or had disappeared. I'd almost given up when I discovered a 20 year-old story on her return to the Gulf Coast buried in a box.

Alexandra LaSalle had graduated from Fairview High School a promising young art student and went straight to the Savannah College of Art and Design to pursue her degree. Her huge, boldly colored oil paintings of sailboats and sea life were unique and groundbreaking for the time, but she didn't finish art school. It didn't give a reason, but a year later she moved to Atlanta where she worked for an advertising firm. She appeared to be doing really well, but inexplicably, she agreed to come back and help Bill Kyser design his new and risky Phoenician complexes that now lined the coast like a wall.

Hurricane Frederick had wiped out almost everything on East End Beach, and Mr. Kyser envisioned his and Mr. Brennan's new developments rolling out in ten phases. They'd be strong enough to face down any storm, and they'd provide a new, more luxurious take on tourism and property ownership in the area—five-star from start to finish.

It was odd to think Ms. LaSalle returned to be part of this huge money-making gamble, and five years later, she was out of the game. I couldn't find anything that explained why or how it happened. She'd virtually disappeared, turning up again later as the owner of a small local art and souvenir shop on Beach Road West. There wasn't a single article that gave me any clues to the reasons.

"How's it going?" Nancy asked.

"Oh, I'm learning a lot about the history of East End Beach. And I found a great feature on Ms. LaSalle. I put it on your desk."

"Yeah, I saw that. Good work. I'm considering dropping in at her shop and talking to her. Maybe if she doesn't see me coming, she'll be more open to an interview. Hey, you know the Kysers pretty well, right?"

"Some of them."

"But you're dating the son. Jack?"

"Umm... maybe I was? It was kind of a strange relationship. And we're not together anymore," I said.

"That explains why I've been seeing you so much lately."

I sort of smiled.

"Well, I'm sorry about that," she gave me a squeeze. "I was going to see if you felt like talking to his dad. A great companion piece would be something on the Phoenicians. You know, reflections on how they changed the area, maybe thoughts on his inspiration. Stuff like that. He brought Alex back. I'd like to hear his side of the story." She dropped her arm. "But I guess you're not interested now."

"No, I'm not." I shuddered, remembering the scene at the hospital and how unhappy he always was to see me. Even if it weren't for my situation with Jack, I didn't want that assignment. "Doesn't he have like a newspaper person or something?"

"A PR department?"

"Yeah."

"Well, of course he does, but that's not what I want. I want more storyteller-type stuff, and since you guys knew each other, I thought he might feel more comfortable talking to you." Nancy crossed her arms and studied her shoes.

"We didn't really know each other," I argued. "Besides, Mr. Kyser's kind of... scary."

Nancy chewed her cheek for a moment and studied me. Then she nodded. "You're right. You're kind of young and inexperienced still. I'll get Sharon to handle it."

And that did it. "No! Don't give it to Sharon! I mean, I could try." I was sick of being told what I was too young to do.

"That's the spirit," she winked. "Take some notes and let me know what you think. And if you meet him at his office, you won't have to worry about seeing his son."

I did take some comfort knowing that much.

"Their offices are over in the Phoenician One complex," Nancy said. "Penthouse suites. I'll ask Curtis to call and work it out so he'll see you. Those guys go way back. It'll be a great learning experience for you." She stopped and scooped the old photos off my desk. "Scan these into the computer, and you can give him the originals. Gifts have a way of softening people up."

"But what if he won't tell me anything?" I said, looking at the pictures. "What if he gets mad."

"Just see if you can get us some talking points, conversation starters. Pretend you're just chatting with an old friend."

"I don't have friends like him."

"Just pretend."

"Right."

* * *

My hands were literally shaking when I arrived at the Phoenician offices, and I didn't know how I was going to take notes without Mr. Kyser seeing it. Luckily Mom had given me a small recorder in case I was too nervous to write. I walked out of the elevator and stopped at the receptionist's desk.

"I've got an appointment to see Mr. Kyser?" I said. "For the paper? Anna Sanders?"

"I'll see if he's available," the receptionist picked up a phone.

A few seconds later, his door opened, and out came Mr. Kyser. I felt a little bead of perspiration slide down my back, but it helped that he wasn't frowning. Yet.

"Anna. Come in." he said as if we were old friends.

My heart was hammering as I followed him into his office. Then I froze. Through a wall of windows I could see the Gulf stretching for miles, turning from turquoise to slightly darker blue to deep marine at the horizon. A few sailboats dotted the expanse.

"Oh, how beautiful!" I gasped, forgetting my fear and walking to the window.

"Hm? Oh, right. I forget how it looks the first time," he said. "You're not from this area."

"No, sir. My mom is, but I grew up in Indiana."

"That's some flat landscape. They grow corn there."

"And apples. Have you been?" I asked.

"I went with my dad once when I was a kid. He was into stock car racing."

I thought of the night after the game, and I decided I never wanted to see another car race as long as I lived. Studying his face, it was amazing how much Jack looked like his dad. It sparked that memory of longing... that I was working hard to get over. I watched as he walked over and sat behind his desk.

"So when Curtis called, he said you're writing for the city paper now," he said. "That's some great experience."

I sat in one of the smaller chairs across from him. "Yes, sir."

"Curtis is a good man. You'll learn a lot."

"I don't ever see him. I work with Nancy Riggs. She's doing a historical insert for the bicentennial and she wanted me to ask you about your work on East End Beach."

He nodded, "I've been thinking about that. I would've thought you all had plenty on me in your archives. It seemed I was always talking to the paper back then. What we were doing, what was coming next."

"I think Nancy wanted something fresh. Like your thoughts looking back. If you're happy with how things turned out. If you'd have done anything differently…"

His expression changed, and I started to grow nervous again. I reached for my bag and pulled out the old pictures. "I found these in the archives." I stood and placed the first one on his desk.

He picked it up and softened a bit. "That's Bryant on one of the Phoenician sites. He must've been twenty years old when this was taken."

"I have one of you and him at the ribbon cutting…" I put it in front of him, and he took one glance before standing up to walk over to a small table that held a decanter of what must've been scotch.

"Would you like some water? Or a Coke?" He poured himself a drink in one of the crystal tumblers on the tray.

"No, thanks," I said. Ms. LaSalle was also in the ribbon-cutting picture, but I acted like I didn't realize. "So I guess, do you mind if I record our interview?"

"Are you writing the story?"

"No. This is for the reporter who will."

He took a drink and walked back to sit behind his desk. "Well, what do you want to know?"

I inhaled and read from my notebook. "What gave you the idea for all these developments? I mean, what made you and Mr. Brennan think you could do something like this?"

"I like how you put it," he said. "I thought the same thing several times when we were getting started. I guess it was youth? We were pretty bold, considering. But it all fell into place for us. We were lucky."

His expression changed as he talked about his work. He became more focused and a little excited. It reminded me of how Julian would get when he told me about one of his new art projects, and my anxiety eased.

I looked down at my notes again. "How would you say the Phoenician developments changed this area?"

"They completely changed the area," he said. "There was nothing down here before Bryant and I got started. Nothing like the year-round residences and ancillary businesses we have now. And what was here had been badly damaged by Frederick."

"Nancy's doing a piece on Ms. LaSalle and her art. She wanted me to ask how she got involved in the developments."

"Alex first helped us when we were seniors…"

"In high school?" I couldn't believe it.

"We were just planning it then. Reading everything we could get our hands on. Bryant's father was in the business, and he gave us some pointers. We had it all mapped out by graduation."

"You're kidding."

"No, we were really focused."

"I can't imagine coming up with something like this at my age," I said. "How'd you do it? Where'd you find the motivation?"

"Farm work in 98 degree heat and 100 percent humidity is very motivating. It forces you to weigh your options."

Again I thought of Julian. "So Ms. LaSalle helped you when you were planning it out?" I asked.

"She drew up our first elevations and sketched out what we were describing. It was amazing to see. She was a really good artist."

"Did you two date?"

He exhaled a quiet laugh. "No. We weren't even friends really."

"But I thought... Why not?"

"Oh, I don't know," he looked away, out the window. "She didn't agree with what we were doing. Thought it would destroy the natural beauty of the area or some hippie nonsense like that."

"But I thought you said you were friends."

"She and Meg were best friends."

"Your wife that died?" He leaned back and for the first time I noticed small lines around his eyes. He seemed tired, and I had completely forgotten to be afraid of him.

"I have this other picture for you," I said. I pulled out the photograph of the group in front of Scoops. He looked at it for several seconds.

"We were seniors when this was taken."

"Lucy looks a lot like her mom," I said, leaning forward.

"Yes. She does."

"It must've been hard losing her like that. Was it a car crash?"

"Right at Christmas," he said. "She lost control of her car. Hit a light pole."

"Oh! I can't even imagine."

He put the picture aside and became serious again. "It was a long time ago. So do you have enough information?"

I nodded. "I think so. Nancy might have someone call and do follow-up. But I think she mainly wanted me to see if you were interested and if there was a connection with the piece she's doing."

"Did you need these?" He picked up the pictures.

"You can have them. I scanned them into the computer at the office," I stood and collected my things. "Thanks for talking to me."

"Thanks for the photos." He rose. "Oh, and thank you for what you said to Lucy. She seems happier than she's been in a while."

"I'm not sure you should thank me," I said. "I couldn't say anything right that day."

He glanced at me, and I saw it. It had been there all along, but I only just saw it now. I felt my eyes widen, and I tried to look down quickly, but he'd seen my expression change.

"Are you okay?" he asked.

"Yes, sir!" I said quickly.

"What's wrong, Anna?"

"Nothing! I was just... thinking about something else."

He didn't seem convinced, but he let it pass. "Hey, about the story."

"What?" I was flustered, but I had to get it together.

"You said this was going to run with a piece on Alex. You're not planning to put us together or anything like that?"

"I don't know what Nancy's planning." I tried to find calm; be a professional. Professionals did not wig out in front of subjects.

"I'd rather avoid that." It sounded like an order.

My eyes flew to his. "I know Nancy wants to do something about her art career with an emphasis on her work here, and I know she's planning to ask her why she stopped painting so abruptly."

"I'd be interested to hear her answer to that question," he said.

"Do you know why she quit?" *If he told me...*

He paused for a second and then looked at his desk.

"That's her business," he said.

207

I wasn't sure how to proceed. Would Nancy want me to pursue this or should I just tell her he might know something? He sat down again.

"I'm surprised you and Jack broke up," he said, successfully throwing me off my game. "You seemed pretty serious, and I was sure you were the reason he wanted to stay at Fairview."

It felt as if he'd kicked the chair out from under me. Imagining Jack wanting to stay for me made my throat hurt and killed the defense I was building against him in my mind.

"Jack never asks for much," he continued. "I figured it didn't matter for a few months longer."

"Yes, sir." I said softly.

"Well, feelings change. It's smart to be sure you're where you want to be." He took a sip of his drink. "Don't make permanent decisions at your age, Anna."

"I thought I might love Jack," I said, wondering why I was telling him this.

He shrugged. "You might also look up one day and realize everything in your life is different. Including your feelings."

"Did that happen to you?"

His finger circled the top of the crystal tumbler that was now empty on his desk. He looked as if he were considering pouring another. "I had other things on my mind at your age."

I studied his light brown hair, thinking of Will. "You married Jack's mom right after high school. I found the announcement in the paper."

He looked up at me, and there it was again. No mistaking it. It was the same expression I'd seen Julian make a hundred times when he was working on a problem or asking me a question. I knew it so well because it was the thing that drew me to him over and over, regardless of how I tried to push him away.

"Nevermind, I've got to go," I said. "Thanks again."

I wanted to get back to the paper office and look through the archives. There had to be a clue somewhere about what had happened. Questions I could never ask directly, but that I was now desperate to find the answers to.

Julian was Mr. Kyser's son. I was sure of it. And that fact could change everything for him. My secret investigation just got a million times more secret.

Chapter 22

When I got back, Nancy was at her desk drumming her pencil. "How'd it go with Kyser," she asked.

"Not bad. There's definitely a story there, but I'm not sure how to find it."

"What are you talking about?"

"Oh!" I realized I'd answered Nancy with the question I'd had in my head. "I meant it was really interesting. He's got a great story."

"Write up your notes, and I'll get one of the reporters to give him a call. Maybe we could give you a dual-byline."

"Oh my god!" *My first real clip!* "Nancy! Thank you!"

She grinned and gave me a hug, but her face went back to tense.

"What's wrong?" I said. "How'd it go with Ms. LaSalle?"

"She won't talk. Said it's all in the past, and she's not interested in being a topic of conversation."

"Did she say why she quit so abruptly?"

"No."

I scrolled through the features I'd been copying onto the computer. It was so much easier than rifling through old papers in the archives, and I was glad I'd been spending so much time scanning them. Finally I arrived at the photo I'd left with Mr. Kyser. The one that clearly unsettled him. It was at the ribbon-cutting ceremony, and I leaned in close to the computer screen staring at Ms. LaSalle.

"What're you doing?" Nancy was right behind me.

I jumped and squealed. "Nancy!"

"We were just talking!" she laughed. "What are you sneaking around here doing?"

"I'm not sneaking. Okay, maybe a little, but look at this. Look at Ms. LaSalle. Is she pregnant in this picture?"

Nancy leaned in. "What's the date on this?"

I looked at the top left corner. She had to be expecting Julian.

"It's the summer before I was born," I said. That would be right about his age.

"What're you getting at, Anna?"

I pulled up another file and started scanning. "It's not in here. Do you have the obit on Meg Kyser?"

"No, but it'll probably be around here." She walked back to the archives room.

"Do you remember when she died?" I asked.

"Well, let's see she had the three kids, but I think they were babies…"

"That's right!" I remembered my first conversation with Bill Kyser. He said the twins were three when it happened. My eyes widened. This was taken before she died!

"What's going on, Anna?"

I was humming now. "I don't know for sure."

"What do you think's going on?" Nancy watched my face, her brows pulled together.

"What if the reason Ms. LaSalle quit painting was because she got pregnant? She never married. What if it had something to do with Julian's father?"

"Like what?" Nancy said.

"I don't know." I couldn't tell her what I was doing, but it was possible she might inadvertently help me.

Nancy pressed her lips together and leaned against the desk. "It's an interesting angle, but after talking to her today, it's not one she'll discuss."

"Could I get Julian's birth certificate?"

"Slow down, Anna. This isn't a gossip rag. Even if that was her reason, it's outside the scope of our article."

"Right," I quickly backpedaled. "You're exactly right. Why would anybody need to know that? I'm sorry."

She smiled and patted my hand. "It's a good instinct. Being pregnant could've been her reason to quit working with Kyser. She was probably keeping some pretty long hours. But I don't see how a baby would cause her to quit painting. And her son's a rising artist now. She clearly encouraged him to pursue that. The dots don't connect."

"You're right. I just got excited. It's an interesting mystery."

I gathered my things to leave. I didn't need to see Julian's birth certificate for my own proof. I'd seen his father's face this afternoon. But Nancy was right. Julian wouldn't have caused Ms. LaSalle to quit painting. There had to be another reason. And why was Ms. LaSalle such a recluse now? I wanted so much to find out what had happened. Maybe I could help her. Maybe I could help all of them somehow.

Chapter 23

My birthday fell on a rainy Wednesday, which was perfect for how I felt about it. I was in no mood for a party. In fact, I'd been meticulously avoiding all social events where I might run into Jack or where any couples were engaging in overt displays of affection. I'd even started eating lunch under a tree by myself at school while listening to my iPod or reading a book. Or both.

It was pretty easy to isolate myself at school, since I'd spent most of the semester wrapped up with Lucy and Jack, and now they were both keeping alternate schedules. It wasn't as depressing as it sounded. Okay, it was pretty depressing, but I was very distracted by my new mystery.

My after-school job consumed all my focus, and anyway, I'd reached the stage where unless people knew you really well, you could sneak birthdays past them. The last bell rang, and I went to my locker eager to gather my books and get to work.

Kids were pushing past me as I spun the lock, and the halls were filled with the usual roar of voices ranging from those hurrying to catch the bus to those staying after for activities. I didn't look around. Finally, I pulled the door open, and a piece of paper dropped to the floor. I leaned down and picked it up. Something was inside the folded sheet, and when I opened it, I found a large yellow chrysanthemum. Familiar handwriting was on the page.

Smile today. –J.

It was from Julian. He remembered my birthday? I looked around but I didn't see him anywhere. The halls were clearing as I pressed the flower to my lips and allowed myself to feel all the feelings I'd been holding at bay. I thought of his kiss, his kisses. Him carrying me. My ring. A flood of warmth filled my chest, and I closed my eyes for a moment, wishing he were here. But I had to wait. I had to be smarter than I'd been so far, and I had to give myself time to be ready.

* * *

Gabi would not let me get through a birthday without some form of communication. She called right before dinner, howling out the song in a voice that would scare babies. "Happy birthday to you…"

"Gabi," I tried to stop the horror.

"Happy birthday to you…"

"Please don't sing."

"Okay! So fill me in. What did Mr. Hot Rich Guy give you for your sweet eighteen?"

Ugh. "You've missed a lot. That is completely over." I pushed through her cries of disbelief and gave her the short version. "We all went to this Halloween hay maze thing, and I got lost and then I wound up kissing Julian. Several times. In a row."

"Hot make-out session?" she laughed. "Yeah, you did! And I'm not even mad. I'm living vicariously now. So who's 'we all'?"

"Me and Jack, Rachel and Brad, Julian and Renee…"

"Renee Barron?"

"Yeah, he's been doing stuff with her again."

"Yikes," I heard Gabi frown. "I think she's what they call 'sex on wheels.'"

"More like sex on anything."

"Reow! Go, Anna!"

"Oh, god, I'm sorry." I cringed. "That was mean."

"Don't apologize to me! She's definitely a problem."

"Not my problem. I'm off the dating scene for the duration." I took a deep breath. "And I've got a story that will curl your hair. What would you say if I told you Julian might be Mr. Kyser's son?"

"I'd say 'What the hell?!'"

"I just know it, Gab. He's got to be." I quickly rehashed the interview in his office, his reactions to the photos, his expression.

"What will you do if you find out it's true?"

I lay back on the bed, a line piercing my brow. "Nothing, I guess."

"So why pursue it?"

"I don't know," I exhaled, rolling onto my side. "It's interesting to me? It's distracting... It helps me forget how bad I feel."

My friend's voice was warm. "Hang in there, banana head."

A little smile touched my lips. Just then I heard my mom calling me for dinner. "I'm still uncovering the details, but I'll let you know if it gets good."

"You'd better! And hey, get over yourself and go out with him."

I paused before hanging up. "What? Who?"

"Julian, you dope."

"Gabi," I breathed, shaking my head. "It's too soon."

"Too soon? You've been friends with Julian two years!"

I rubbed my forehead hard. "That's part of the problem. I love being his friend. And the other part, well, I'm still not over Jack."

Fight as I might, I still had the occasional dream of being in his arms, and I still missed how he made me feel.

"Jack, schmack. Julian's the one."

"I gotta go," I said. "The parents demand their birthday time, too."

I ran downstairs with my thoughts on Julian. If Mr. Kyser were his dad, that would make him and Jack half brothers. Brothers. Could that be my problem? They both shared some gene that pulled me in like a tractor beam?

All I knew is I would not ruin things with Julian. Like Mr. Kyser said, I would wait and be sure of my feelings first.

* * *

The cool thing about having a school-related job was being able to leave during lunch on work errands. On Monday I used my work excuse to run to the satellite courthouse to search through birth certificates. Mary Ott had been the clerk there for years, and before that, she'd taught at Fairview Elementary School, where my mother had attended. When we moved back, she was one of the first people I met, and I knew she wouldn't mind me poking around in the old files. When I arrived, she was as chatty and friendly as ever.

"Anna Sanders! How's your mamma?" Mary knew the southern drill.

"Just fine, Mrs. Ott. Did she tell you I've been working at the paper in Fairview?" I asked.

"No! That sounds like a lot of fun. Is that why you're here? Shouldn't you be at school?" Mrs. Ott smiled at me like I was a misbehaving first grader.

"Oh, it's OK," I said. "I've got a pass. I need to look through some of the old records. Birth certificates. Can you help me?"

She led me to a room where the walls were lined with filing cabinets. It was dusty and smelled like a library, and each of the long drawers was labeled by the year.

"These are the public records up until we started keeping them on the computer," she explained. "Older stuff is in the basement or on microfilm. Some things have been sent to the county seat."

"I bet I can find what I'm looking for," I said, kneeling in front of a drawer labeled with my birth year. I started in the middle, pulling out the old files. The first one I found was a listing for the sale of an old home with property on Port Hogan Road to Kyser-Brennan equities. They must've been buying up as much beachfront property as they could get back then, but Port Hogan Road was on the opposite end of the island from where the Phoenician developments were located. Why would they want something so far away?

I let the documents slide back into their hanging file and moved further back in the drawer. Everything was mixed in, and I wondered how they found anything in here until I saw the pattern. Birth records were in red folders.

After a few more tries, I found it. Julian's birth certificate. The lighting was dim, and it was hard to figure out where the vital information was located in the small boxes. I didn't realize so much was crammed onto such a small sheet of paper. Finally, I found it. In the space for mother it listed Alexandra Marie LaSalle. Under father it was... blank. *Blank?* Was it possible to leave the father space on a birth certificate blank? I had no idea, but it was done in this case.

I sat back on my heels and sighed. *Now what?* I couldn't prove anything if the birth certificate was blank, and short of Ms. LaSalle's coming out and saying it, or of some desire for a paternity test on Mr. Kyser's part, there would never be a way to know for sure. Not that it mattered, of course. But I was just so close... even if it was just for me, I wanted to see this through.

For a few moments I chewed my lip, wondering what a good journalist would do. *Talk.* Journalists talked. I dropped the file back into the drawer and closed it. Mrs. Ott was busy with another visitor when I left, so I waved and ran out to my car. If I didn't hurry, I'd be late.

* * *

My plan was forming in my mind as I packed my book bag. The last thing I expected was to look up and see Jack. I froze. It had almost been a month. I was just getting my confidence back, and here he was walking in my direction, stirring up all the old feelings I'd been working so hard to forget.

As usual, he was dressed in khakis that fit perfectly, and today he wore a blue oxford that made his eyes glow. I tried not to stare, but I stood unable to move as he walked over to me.

"Dad said you came by his office."

The sound of his voice actually hurt. How was it possible that my feelings were stronger now than when I saw him all the time? "Nancy wanted me to talk to him for the bicentennial insert." I managed to say.

"How'd it go?"

I shrugged. "Fine. I was nervous at first, but he was pleasant enough." I wondered what Jack would say about my suspicions.

He waited a few seconds longer, his eyes flickering over my face. "How've you been?"

"Good," I said. Not as good as I'd wanted to believe, but he didn't need to know that.

He nodded. "I was just picking up some final paperwork. See you around."

"See ya," I said softly, watching him walk away. Again I wanted to bang my head against the locker. Hard.

I thought I'd made such progress. Then he walked in and all I wanted was for him to pin me against the wall. My teeth clenched, and I wished I were far away where I could smash something or scream really loudly.

My brow was lined, and I was lost in thought when I heard Julian calling me. *Great.* Feelings for him would remain on hold it seemed. But as he ran closer, he reminded me of what I was doing. Julian might be an artist and dress like a post-punk rocker, but his expression was the same one I'd left in the boardroom yesterday. It was exactly how Mr. Kyser had looked when the pieces snapped together.

What would Julian say if he knew his dad was Bill Kyser? Or that Jack was his half brother? He might be angry, and they might deny it. No, the identity of Julian's dad was a bombshell I would never drop.

"What's going on under all those curls?" he laughed. "That was one serious expression."

"I thought I might visit your mom today," I said, closing my locker. We walked together to the exit. "Nancy's doing a piece on her art, and I thought maybe I could help her with it."

Julian shook his head. "Not a good idea. Mom quit the business way back. She never talks about it anymore."

"But why?" I studied his expression. "She encourages you so much. Don't you think she misses it?"

"I don't know," he said, holding the heavy metal door. "I always figured something happened in art school. I just give her space."

"Think she'll talk to me?"

He shrugged. "She's always liked you, and after that night at the hospital, she said something about you being very sweet."

"Speaking of sweet," I stopped and faced him. "Thank you for my birthday flower. That was very sweet."

He smiled and reached over to move one of my curls out of my face. "I hated seeing you alone on your birthday."

Jack might be stuck in my head, but at that moment, Julian's arms were the ones I wanted around me. So much. Instead I exhaled, and we resumed walking. "So I was going to drop by and talk to your mom, but I'll try not to make her mad."

"Why bother her? I mean, she's not painting anymore. Why start something?"

"I won't," I said, thinking.

I never wanted to make Julian's mom mad, but if I could get some idea of her feelings, maybe she was as lonely as Mr. Kyser was. Maybe I could help them find their way back to each other, and maybe if that happened, together they could fix whatever had damaged Jack's family so much.

I thought of Lucy having a mother again... I thought of Julian having a dad...

"I'll be careful," I said, sunny optimism filling my chest as I climbed into my car.

Chapter 24

Ms. LaSalle was dressed in a filmy, knee-length sundress, and when I arrived at her store, she was carrying a huge cardboard box from the front porch inside. Several large boxes along with an assortment of smaller ones were stacked around the front entrance, which was decorated with whimsical stained-glass ornaments and wind chimes. Her long hair swished down her back as she disappeared around the corner. Everything about her and her space was breezy and carefree. A white boardwalk led to the entrance, and I parked the car and got out just in time for her to reemerge and grab another large box.

"Can I help you?" I asked, trotting up the walk.

"Anna," she smiled. "Sure, you're just in time for Christmas delivery. It's the big one. Half the time I can't even remember what I've ordered, so lots of surprises. Just carry the smaller ones. I don't want you getting hurt."

I was glad I'd worn pants and a tee. We would get hot carrying boxes, even in November. "But you're carrying the big ones."

"I've got more practice. Here." She handed me a small one. "I think that has a new shipment of jewelry in it."

I followed her inside the store, which was divided in half. One side displayed paintings, pottery, and all sorts of art, including a nice selection of Julian's work. The other side was woven jewelry, clothes, and souvenirs ranging from the standard sea shells to stained-glass windows and items from local collectors.

"I love your store," I said, placing the small box on the counter.

"Thanks!" She smiled. "I haven't seen you around lately. What's going on?"

"Just school, work. You know. Stuff like that."

"You have a job?" she asked.

"Well, it's kind of part-job, part-school, I guess. I'm hoping to get a journalism scholarship, so I'm doing an internship at the paper in Fairview."

She stopped and looked at me for a second. "With Nancy Riggs?"

"Yeah." I picked up a small ring that was lying on the counter. She picked up a box cutter and opened one of the larger boxes.

"Oh, look at this," she said pulling out a piece of Raku pottery.

"Who did that?" I asked.

"I have a friend who makes these. Isn't it beautiful?"

"Yeah, it is." I twirled the ring in my fingers. It was glass that had been molded and shaped into a ring and it had streaks of color melted through the band. "I really like this."

"That came from the Hot Shop in East End Beach. The glass-blowing studio? They make some really pretty pieces over there. Have you been?"

"No." I waited, trying to decide how to broach the subject. "Julian never told me you were an artist."

"*Were* is the key word there," she smiled.

"But you still keep up with your artist friends."

"Well, if I can sell their pieces, I try to, but that's all really. This Raku pottery is flying off the shelves, and I know a guy who's been making these since we were in art school." She laughed quietly. "I was hopeless at Raku pottery."

"Really? Why?"

"I kept breaking my pots. See, you work with very high heat, and they shatter so easily. I was much better with the brush."

"Mom said they have some of your paintings in the old Magnolia Hotel. I haven't seen them, but I heard you were very good."

"I liked to paint when I was younger. It was sort of my escape." She slid a piece of her long, dark hair behind her shoulder. "Or my protection."

"I can understand that," I said. "It's kind of how I feel about my journal."

She smiled and continued pulling out plastic packages of shark teeth and woven bracelets. "I kept a journal once. I was just starting art school, and I wanted to capture all my thoughts and experiences."

"Do you still have it?"

"No, I lost it a long time ago." A brief flash of something crossed her face. "I should probably try to find it."

I held a package of Swarovski crystal beads to the light. "These are gorgeous."

"I gave a few of those to Julian for that ring he was making," she said. "Did you like it?"

I hadn't worn it today. I'd decided to save it for special occasions. "It was so beautiful. Julian's really talented. I guess he got that from you?"

She shrugged.

"You know, Nancy wanted to get a photographer over there to take pictures of your paintings. She really wanted to do something nice and positive about your art and how it influenced this area."

She shook her head. "I have nothing to say to her, and I'm not interested in dredging all that up. No one even remembers me that way now."

"You make it sound like it's something bad. I think it's neat that you were a painter and that you helped with the Phoenicians."

"What do you know about that?" Her suddenly sharp tone made me nervous.

"Uhh... I saw some old articles and pictures," I said. "And I talked to Mr. Kyser the other day. Nancy wanted to do a piece on him also."

"This is what I mean." She slapped a package on the counter. "It starts with one thing and then it goes to another."

I tried changing my approach. "I found a picture of you guys in high school," I said. "It was taken at Scoops. I hardly recognized the place."

She calmed down a little. "Things used to be so different here."

"That's what Mr. Kyser said. He said you weren't too happy about his ideas."

"Really." Her eyebrow arched. "What else did he say?"

"Not much. I wondered why you would quit painting. I can't imagine not writing."

She stopped sorting and gazed out the window. "I couldn't do it anymore after... it just turned my stomach."

"After...?"

"Hey, I never told you I really appreciated you staying with me at the hospital that night," she said. "It was sweet."

"I was glad to do it."

"I think it meant a lot to Julian, too," she smiled at me then turned her back and continued unpacking. "You know, you can just call me Alex if you want. And don't worry about all that 'yes ma'am' business."

"OK. But I don't think I can call you Alex. It's too weird."

"Aren't you from up north?"

"Indiana."

"So where'd all these Old South manners come from?"

"Peer pressure," I said, sliding the plastic baggies apart on the counter. "Actually, my mom's from Fairview. She just moved away when she was in elementary school. So I guess it's her fault."

"Listen, Anna. Ugly things happened back then. It's best to leave the past… past."

I looked down, unsure of what to say. I thought of that night at the hospital and how Mr. Kyser had looked at her. Julian's mom was so beautiful. I thought of my idea, of helping them get back together, helping Julian…

"I think he's still in love with you," I said.

She paused. "Who."

"Mr. Kyser. He saw your picture, and I think… well, he got up and fixed a drink."

"Anna. Don't."

"But what about Julian?" I said. Then I jumped, biting my lip. That just slipped out.

"What about Julian?"

"I-I just meant…" I couldn't meet her gaze. I was taking a huge risk, but maybe it could help them?

"I don't know what you're thinking," she said, sounding angry, "but just stop right there."

My hands were shaking now. "Oh, Ms. LaSalle," I said, blinking fast. "I don't want to make you mad. You're just so pretty, and I wish you weren't alone."

"I'm alone because I choose to be."

"And Mr. Kyser… I always thought he was so mean,

229

but he's really not. He's just so sad. I don't think he wants to be alone either. I think he wants to be with you."

"Did he tell you that?"

"No, but…" My heart was racing. "I didn't tell him what I know."

"What do you know?"

I looked down. *Here goes…* "That Julian's his son."

She simply stared at me, but I could tell by her expression I was right. "I'm not talking about this with you or anyone else," she said quickly.

"But why won't you be with him?" I said, following her to the back of the shop. "I saw you at the hospital. You still love him, too."

"You need to go. Now. And I'd appreciate it if you wouldn't say anything to Julian about this."

"No! Of course not—I never would." I met her eyes then, and she looked as much angry as afraid. "I just wish… I wish you would."

"This conversation is over," she said.

I nodded, backing slowly away and putting the ring on the counter again. She wouldn't look at me, and I knew I'd messed up. I hadn't helped anyone, and I'd done just what I'd told Julian I wouldn't do.

I exhaled in frustration. I'd leave them alone. I'd drop the whole thing. I just couldn't understand being in love with someone and maintaining such a long separation. Couldn't Ms. LaSalle move past whatever bad things had happened? It didn't seem right for her to punish herself or Mr. Kyser. Or Julian for that matter. I didn't understand, and I wished I knew why.

Chapter 25

The next afternoon at the paper, I decided to spend the day scanning pictures and forget the Kyser story altogether. I did not expect to be called into Mr. Waters' office the minute I arrived. Nancy was already there, and Mr. Waters was not smiling.

"I got a call from Bill Kyser today saying I've got reporters snooping into his private life," he said. "This is a small-town paper, ladies. Guys like Bill Kyser can put us out of business."

Nancy spoke up. "I don't know what he's all fired up about, Curtis. Anna just asked him a few questions about developing the Phoenicians and the history of the area. Right, Anna?"

They both turned to look at me. My mouth dropped open. I knew what I'd done yesterday had crossed a line, but I didn't expect this. And I didn't know what to say now.

"Well? What do you have to say for yourself?" Mr. Waters demanded.

I felt my face turning red. I couldn't even remember what day I'd talked to Mr. Kyser, much less what I'd asked him. It seemed like we'd talked as much about my personal life as his.

"I don't know, Mr. Waters." I stammered. "I just asked him about his inspiration, and I had some old pictures I gave him. Some of them had his wife and Ms. LaSalle in them."

Curtis Waters leaned back in his chair and chewed on his pencil. Nancy pressed her lips together and looked down at the carpet. After a few moments of silence he spoke.

"Sounds like somebody touched a nerve. Only two times people call a paper: when they're in the wrong and they're scared we'll print it, or when we've made a mistake and printed something wrong. And we haven't printed anything yet."

He rocked in his chair a few times. "So what do you think, Anna?"

My eyes widened. "About what?"

"Think he's hiding something? Something that matters?"

"I don't know," I lied.

"Well, what's he so upset about?" Mr. Waters growled. "You not talking because you're dating that little Kyser? What's it, John? Jack?"

"Jack," I said. "No, sir. We're not dating."

He sat forward. "So tell me what you know. You must've uncovered something when you talked to Bill or he wouldn't be calling me to try and put a lid on it."

"I really don't know. I mean, I don't have anything definite, and I promised I wouldn't say anything," I rambled.

"Promised who? Kyser?"

I looked up at him for the first time since our meeting began. "Mr. Waters, I can't tell you anything else about it."

Silence again. Then he nodded.

"All right," he snapped. "But your job in this office is to assist in the newsroom. If you want to go off and play Miss Investigative Reporter, that's fine. Good luck to you. But when you start pestering the most powerful man in town and don't let your editor and publisher in on it, I can't cover your ass."

I looked down again. *I will not cry.* "Yes, sir."

232

Nancy tried to rescue me. "Curtis, I think Anna might have gotten a little excited about some of the archive materials. Some of the old pictures with Kyser and Alex LaSalle."

Mr. Waters thought a few moments. "What's so exciting about that? Everybody knows those two worked together. Why would that warrant an angry call?"

He paused again, then without looking at me, he said, "Monitor it, Nan, and if you uncover anything, let me know. And if this student intern thing isn't working out, well, let me know about that too."

He swiveled his chair around and we were dismissed.

We crossed the newsroom in silence. My insides were like Jell-O, and I wanted to cry at the thought he might fire me. I loved my job here. I needed it for college, and for now, it was all I had keeping me going. When we reached Nancy's office, she pulled me inside.

"What did you do?" she said quietly.

"Nothing!" I tried to keep calm. I wasn't fired yet.

"You did something," Nancy insisted.

I closed my eyes and inhaled. "I went to see Ms. LaSalle yesterday. I thought I could casually talk to her about her art and stuff and maybe help you."

"And?"

"I'm not sure exactly how it happened, but we got on the subject of Mr. Kyser, and I might've said something about him being in love with her."

Nancy stood and shut her door. "Did he tell you that?"

"No, but it's so obvious."

"Obvious in what way?" She sat behind her desk, and the look on her face boosted my confidence.

I scooted forward in my chair. "Remember when Brad and Julian were in that accident, and Julian was in the hospital?"

"Oh, yeah," Nancy nodded. "The quarterback miraculously escaped without a scratch."

"But Julian didn't. He lost consciousness and had to stay overnight. I was there, and at one point, so was Bill Kyser. And I walked in on them. He was holding Ms. LaSalle in his arms, and I heard him say something about letting him take care of this. Like he was talking about the bills."

"The bills?" Nancy frowned. "What could that mean?"

"I don't know, but it must mean something."

We were quiet for a second.

"Just watch it," Nancy said. "I like you, Anna. You've been a big help to me, and I'd hate to lose you over this."

I nodded and left Nancy's office. My fear had slowly turned into anger. I replayed the scene in my head, and I couldn't remember asking a single personal question when I was in Mr. Kyser's office. I couldn't believe he'd call and get me in trouble like that. Getting fired from my one internship would kill my scholarship dreams, and there would be no way I could list it on my transcript. I wanted to go over and confront him about it, and the more I thought about it, the more determined I became.

I left Nancy a note saying I had to run an errand and drove to the Phoenician offices. Stepping off the elevator, I stopped again at the receptionist's desk.

"I was hoping I could catch Mr. Kyser," I said. "It's Anna Sanders from the paper again?"

"He's already gone for the day, Miss Sanders," the lady smiled.

"Was he going home?"

"I have no idea what Mr. Kyser does when he leaves here."

"Right."

I got back in the elevator, and as I rode down the 14 floors, I tried to decide what to do. I could drive to their house. But what if I saw Jack again?

I couldn't let that stop me. I was going to get to the bottom of this, and I was doing it now.

* * *

It'd been weeks since I'd been to the enormous home on Peninsula Avenue, and I still felt as intimidated as ever pulling into the driveway. The Jeep was there, and my stomach clenched at the sight. The Audi was also there. This was a crazy idea. What had I been thinking? Did I actually plan to confront Mr. Kyser about getting me in trouble? I must've been suffering from temporary insanity.

I was just about to restart the car when the front door opened, and Jack walked out. He was wearing jeans and a grey tee, and I could see the lines of his shoulders through the thin cotton fabric. Gorgeous. My lips remembered touching that skin. I could still taste it. I put my head on the steering wheel and peeked at him through the space. It was too late to run, and my eyes followed him as he came closer and tapped on the glass.

"What're you doing here?" he asked as I lowered the window.

"I was just thinking the same thing."

"Lucy's down at Months Bay. Dad's inside…"

235

"I should go," I said.

"Hang on," he lifted the handle to open the door and helped me out. "Take a walk with me?"

My brain was screaming no, but my mouth said yes. I got out and followed him down the driveway and out to the beach. I had no idea what was coming, all I knew was something sick inside me wanted to find out.

He stopped and turned to me, the wind pushing his hair around his face. My fingers itched to touch it, slide it off his forehead.

"I've been thinking about you since yesterday." He looked down before speaking again. "I've had something I wanted to tell you for a while. Since Jesse's. That night. But I didn't know if I wanted to say it out loud."

My cheeks grew hot. I remembered the night he was talking about. It was the night he'd wanted to sleep with me. "Okay?"

"Being with you was more than I expected," he said. "And it's possible... I mean, I was thinking it would be very easy for me to fall for you."

"I don't understand. Are you saying...?"

"I wasn't finished."

"Oh." My throat grew painfully tight.

"I mean, I feel these things, but you're just so young. And I'm dealing with all this shit."

"I'm eighteen now," I interrupted, thinking of my sad little birthday.

"I didn't know... Happy birthday."

I nodded, looking down. "It's okay. I didn't really feel like a party."

"Anna." He exhaled and looked away. "I'm finished with school. That's why I was there yesterday. I took my last exam and in two weeks, I'm moving to New

Orleans. I'll focus on college, I'll be working with Will... I won't have a lot of time."

I couldn't speak. My insides felt dead. This was it. He was leaving, and after all the time I'd spent doing everything in my power to forget about him, it still hurt hearing him say it.

"It doesn't matter, I guess." He exhaled and looked into the wind. "I just didn't want you to think it didn't mean anything to me."

We were standing just steps apart, and my hand instinctively rose to touch his cheek. It was scratchy. A little stubble. "I know. You said it wasn't a good idea."

"But you kept talking about books." He stepped back and smiled. "I told you I have a thing for librarians."

"You hated every book we read."

He passed his hand over his cheek where I'd just touched him, and my heart ached. I wondered if this was the last time I'd see him, the last memory I'd have of us together.

"It really is for the best," he said.

"You always say that." I crossed my arms at my waist and turned to head back to the house. I felt a light touch on my shoulder and looked back. He took a quick step forward and kissed my forehead, right at my hairline.

"Goodbye, Anna. Take care of yourself."

My chest tightened, but I didn't want to cry in front of him. I blinked a little smile and nodded. "Good luck with college."

I didn't want to talk to his dad anymore. I couldn't care about that right now. But before I climbed into my car, I looked back and saw Jack had followed me. He was standing in the doorway. I pulled the door closed and drove away, pain knotted in my chest.

At home I went inside, walked straight to my room, closed my door and sat on my bed. I couldn't tell how many minutes passed as I stared blankly at the wall. I could only think one thing: It was over.

My insides were completely still.

Finally, I got up and washed my face, changed into my pajamas, and went back to my bed. I lay on my side for several minutes staring at the wall. I didn't know what to do to make the tears start. I was ready for the gut-wrenching sobs to begin, but my emotions wouldn't cooperate. My feelings never acted right. I rolled onto my back and looked at the ceiling for a long time.

* * *

Sleep must have come, because the next time I opened my eyes it was daylight. Gabi was texting me about the annual Key West marathon and demanding to know the latest news on the formerly secret mystery.

I rolled onto my stomach and sent back a message describing how I'd almost gotten fired. She texted a rant about the suppression of information, and I defended Nancy at least, explaining how she'd given me the assignment to interview Jack's dad.

How did that go? Were your knees knocking? she texted back.

Practically. Had to bring a recorder. I typed, and then I gasped. "Oh my god!" I whispered. Just as fast I typed that I had to go.

I had the whole thing recorded! Jack's dad couldn't accuse me of asking personal questions because now I could prove I hadn't. I threw the covers back and jumped up, pulling on jeans and a long-sleeved tee. I threw my phone in my bag and grabbed the little recorder off my desk. Dashing across the hall, I raced to the bathroom to splash water on my face. Then I ran down the stairs and grabbed Mom's car keys.

"Whoa, hang on there. Where's the fire?" Dad was sitting at the bar holding the paper.

"Sorry, Dad! I've got to go."

"Hold it." He looked stern. "What you've got to do is tell me where you're running off to and when you'll be back."

I didn't have time for this sudden parental over-involvement. "It's paper business. I'm working on a historical piece with Nancy, and I just remembered I need to interview this person. I won't be gone long."

"Got your phone?"

"Yep! Back in a few hours!"

* * *

As I raced down the beach road toward Dolphin Shores, I realized I had no idea what I was doing. I was driving toward Julian's house, so I figured I'd start there. And of the two of them, I'd likely make more progress with his mom. She had to have called Mr. Kyser and told him what I'd said about Julian, and then he called Mr. Waters and accused me of snooping.

But I wasn't going to tell their secret, and she *had* to smooth things over for me at the paper. I didn't want to use the recording, I wanted her to agree to help me. And I wanted her to do it because we were friends.

I was still thinking about what I would say to her when I turned the car into Ms. LaSalle's little shop and ran up the boardwalk. It was closed and all the lights were off. I ran around back and peeped in the window. Nothing.

I got back in the car and drove to Julian's house a few blocks away, but when I arrived, Mr. Kyser's silver Audi was parked in the driveway. I paused wondering what this meant and what I should do. I decided to slip in through Julian's garage workshop and see if I could tell what was going on.

The door was open, so I walked in past several unfinished pieces. I heard their voices inside grow loud and then taper off, so I slipped to the door and pushed it open a crack to peek inside. There was no sign of Julian anywhere.

"You've got to go," she said. "What if Julian comes back and you're here? What will I tell him?"

"The truth?" Mr. Kyser's voice was urgent, but heartbreaking, too. I could hear how much he loved her. "We really can't keep going like this, Lex. If a teenage girl can figure it out, it's just a matter of time—"

"Anna's just smart and sensitive," Ms. LaSalle interrupted. "She picks up on things. Besides, Julian is used to not having a father. If we tell him now—"

"What? You're afraid you'll lose him?"

"I don't know," she said softly.

"Look, I know I agreed to this, but I want to know my son," Mr. Kyser's voice was pleading. "I want us to be together."

Ms. LaSalle looked down and her long hair slid across her face. Mr. Kyser went to her and pulled her into his arms. She didn't fight him as he lowered his head and kissed her. His hands gently cupped her cheeks, and it was so gentle and passionate and earnest. I started to turn away, but she broke away from him first.

"It's been so long," he said softly. "We could try—"

"No. We lost that chance when she died."

"I don't believe that," he said. "Why does it have to be that way? Why do you make it that way?"

"Because it's how I feel. I can close my eyes and forget her for a minute, five minutes, but she's always there waiting to come back and remind me of what I did. What we did."

"She's gone, Lex. The only thing reminding you is you."

Julian's mom shook her head, "It won't work. Too much has happened."

"So what's the point if we simply grow old alone?" He was back to pleading.

"You and I are not supposed to be together," she insisted.

"How can you say that? If things had been different, we would have easily been together. It was always going to happen. It started the day I came to get you in Atlanta."

"Oh, god. If only I'd stayed in Atlanta," she sighed. "Things would be so different."

"You couldn't stay there. You weren't happy there." He went back and pulled her into his arms again. "Remember your first day back, when we sat on the beach and talked? I'll never forget it. You can't say that didn't mean anything to you."

"Why are you doing this?" she asked. "Why are you here? Everything was fine, and now you're just making it hard again."

"Is it hard for you? I can never tell."

She looked up at him, and tears were in her eyes. He kissed her again, and this time she lifted her hands and slid them around his neck. *She was kissing him back!*

I wanted to cheer, but I covered my mouth and stepped back from the door. A noise caused me to spin around. Julian was walking into the garage.

"Anna!" He said, smiling at me. "What are you doing here? Whose car is that?"

"Julian!" I spoke as loudly as I could and pushed the door open I'd just been peeking through. "I was... umm... Oh! Remember how I told you I was helping Nancy with that piece on your mom?"

"Why are you yelling?" he frowned.

"I'm not yelling. Am I talking loud?" I tried to look confused as I continued near-shouting. I was sure I was acting completely psychotic. "Sorry. Well, you know how your mom helped with the Phoenician complexes and all?"

"Yeah." Julian winced. "Damn, girl, tone it down."

"Well, Nancy asked if I would interview Mr. Kyser and her together. I was just coming out here to show him my ring. I told him about how beautiful it was, and he wanted to see it." I'd made the whole story up, but hopefully the two inside would understand and play along.

Julian smiled and lifted my hand. "Jack's dad's here? And you're showing him the ring I made you? That sounds promising."

My voice tapered off as we studied it. "Yeah. It was the first thing I thought of."

"I'm glad." He straightened it on my finger, and with our hands together, his tattoo and my ring appeared to be flying to each other.

I slid my finger over his mark feeling comforted. One wouldn't give me a chance, but the other was only waiting for a chance. I swallowed the tightness in my throat. I was so ready for my heart to be ready for Julian.

"Anyway, I think we can show him now," I said.

Inside the house, Mr. Kyser was flipping through a magazine on the table and Ms. LaSalle was in the kitchen putting water in a kettle.

"Hey, guys. Here's the ring I was telling you about," I said walking over to Mr. Kyser. He frowned at me. "Remember? The ring Julian made for me? Isn't it gorgeous?"

"It's very nice. Helen Freed?" Mr. Kyser said.

"Yep." Julian stepped up beside me. "She described her technique to me, and I played around with some variations. I'm Julian."

He held out his hand to Mr. Kyser. Mr. Kyser paused and looked at him. Then he shook Julian's hand. It was all I could do to keep from making a sound.

"Bill Kyser," he said, clearing his throat. "I've seen you around."

I looked into the kitchen, and Ms. LaSalle was frozen watching them. For a moment I thought she might reconsider telling Julian the truth. Then she spoke.

"Julian, would you do me a favor? I was going to open the store, but when these guys got here, I lost track of the time. Would you mind?"

"Need me to open it for you?" he said.

"Please. If you're not doing anything?"

"Sure, Mom." Julian walked over to the fridge and grabbed a soft drink. As he passed her, she ran the back of her hand down his arm.

"Thanks," she smiled at him.

The three of us waited in silence until we were sure Julian was gone. As soon as the door closed, I exhaled a long breath and dropped onto the couch.

"What are you doing here? Why were you back there?" Ms. LaSalle snapped at me.

I was stunned by her tone. I couldn't believe she would be stern with me after I just saved her neck.

"I wanted to talk to you," I said. "And I wasn't sure if Julian was here."

"You really are an annoying little snoop, Anna." Mr. Kyser agreed.

"That's not fair! You lied about me," I said. "You almost got me fired, and I want to know why."

"Lied about you?" Ms. LaSalle asked.

"Mr. Waters called me into his office yesterday and yelled at me for asking him a bunch of personal questions." I pointed to Mr. Kyser. "Only I didn't ask you any personal questions. You asked *me* a bunch of personal questions."

"I don't know what you're talking about." Mr. Kyser dismissed me.

"This internship means a lot to me. It's helping me with college, and now I might lose it."

"Calm down, Anna." Ms. LaSalle said. "Nobody's trying to get you in trouble. I'll call and smooth things over if you like."

"I'd like you to be honest," I said. "I'd like you to tell Julian the truth."

"That's not going to happen," Ms. LaSalle muttered.

"Why not?" I turned to Mr. Kyser. "Julian's a great guy. He deserves to know who his dad is. He deserves what you can give him."

Mr. Kyser looked down and didn't speak. Ms. LaSalle turned her back on both of us and put her hands on the small table. She was quiet for several minutes. I knew now that she was the reason Julian didn't know, and nothing I could say would change her mind. After several more seconds she turned around.

"I'll make a deal with you," she said.

Mr. Kyser and I both stared at her waiting.

"I'll give Nancy the interview," she continued. "I won't talk about anything personal, but I'll answer her questions, and I'll make up some reason why I stopped painting. Burnout or something. I'll tell her you convinced me to talk to her."

"But… Why would you do that?" I asked.

"Because I need you to trust me," she said. "I need you to believe me when I say that not telling Julian is for the best."

I didn't know what to say. On the one hand, her agreeing to do the interview with Nancy and smoothing things over was the whole reason I'd come here. But I felt like I was getting what I wanted by selling out my friend.

"I don't know," I said. "I mean, what about Julian?"

Mr. Kyser stepped in.

"Come by my office Tuesday." He led me to the door. "We'll talk more then."

I looked at him, and his expression had changed. It was softer somehow. I had no idea what to make of that.

"OK." I said. "I guess you want to be alone."

"I need to get down to the store," Ms. LaSalle said, picking up her bag. "It's not fair to make Julian work when he wasn't planning to."

"I'll go and hang out with him," I said. "I mean, if you two want to talk."

"There's nothing more to say," Ms. LaSalle said.

"Lexy, please." Mr. Kyser spoke.

I went to the door. "See you Tuesday."

* * *

I ran down to the car and drove back to Ms. LaSalle's shop. I was less ready than ever to be alone with Julian after what had happened at Jack's house. But I hoped by being here, Mr. Kyser could convince his mom to see her feelings. I walked into the small building and found him sitting on the bead table stringing a bracelet.

"That's pretty," I walked over and gently touched the bright turquoise beads.

"Thanks," he smiled. "Mom's been keeping kits like this around since I was a kid."

"For you?" I smiled back. He nodded. Then he gestured to my hand.

"I like you wearing my ring."

I slid it around on my finger, loving the way it sparkled. "It's my favorite piece of jewelry."

He reached forward and took my hand, holding it gently. "Want something to match it? A necklace or something?"

"I saw Jack yesterday," I blurted. Somebody had to be honest to him. "We ended things. For good this time."

His brow creased, and I could tell he was concerned. "Are you okay?"

"I've been better. At least I've gotten used to feeling this way."

He released my hands and went back to the piece he'd been working on when I arrived. Silently he tied off the clasps and then stood to hang it on one of the little display racks by the drawers. I walked over to the counter and picked up the glass ring I'd been holding when I talked to his mom. He went around to the other side and leaned on the counter facing me.

"Still aceing algebra?" I asked.

"Yeah," he said. "But I miss my old tutor."

I slipped his ring off my finger. "I think I might save wearing this for later."

"Later?" Our eyes met, and it hurt to think I might ever disappoint him.

"When I look at it, it feels like it means so much." I closed my fingers around the delicate piece. "And I'm not ready."

"It doesn't have to mean so much just yet," Julian inched his finger into my palm and took the ring out, sliding it back to its spot on my hand. I looked at it again. It was so beautiful.

"But don't you see?" My eyes went to his. "It does to me."

He didn't stop me slipping it off again. "Okay," he said. "If that's how you feel. Keep it somewhere safe."

"I will."

I left the small shop and was in my car when I saw Ms. LaSalle walking up. Her expression gave nothing away, and I wondered what had happened after I left. I only waved as I pulled onto the road to my house.

Chapter 26

Nancy was beaming the next time I arrived at the office. She came around the counter grinning like she was going to pin a medal on me. "What did you do?" she said.

I dropped my bag behind the counter, brow creased. "What?"

"I just got off the phone with Ms. Alexandra LaSalle. She'll be very happy to talk to me about her art and when can we get together."

"You're kidding!"

"She said it was because of you."

"Me?" I acted bewildered while trying to think of a plausible explanation. "Well, I'm friends with her son, you know."

"Right."

"I was visiting over the weekend, and we just got to talking. I guess she realized she was being too sensitive."

"Well, whatever happened, big points for Anna."

"Thanks."

"I'll be interviewing her next week. Wish me luck!"

"Good luck!"

* * *

I had no clue what to expect at my meeting with Mr. Kyser. Would he threaten me? Try to bribe me? I decided I'd repeat my position that it should be them, Julian's parents, who told him the truth. This little messenger was not about to be killed. Or lose my friend. I was uneasy as I turned the car toward East End Beach and made my way to Phoenician One.

The receptionist recognized me on sight. I walked in, and she told me who I was and to take a seat. I fidgeted with a magazine while I waited, and after what seemed an eternity, he appeared.

"Anna. Come in." He said, all business.

I walked into his stunning office and sat in the small chair I'd occupied at our previous meeting. He walked around his desk and sat.

"I wanted to talk to you because I know you're smart and you care about your friends," he began. "I get that, and I care about them, too. But I have something to discuss with you. Off the record."

Here we go. "Okay."

He reached down to open a large drawer in his desk and pulled out three thick journals. One was leather-bound, and the other two were covered in colorful fabric. Then he also reached into the drawer again and pulled out what looked like a present wrapped in brown paper with a green foil ribbon tied gaily around it. He handed the present to me first.

"This is from Lucy. She wanted me to give it to you. Christmas present or something."

"Thanks." Suddenly I felt awful for neglecting our friendship. Even if I was sure she'd been completely occupied with B.J.

"These are the reason I wanted to see you here. Alone." He picked up the three books and placed them in a stack in front of me. I was mystified.

"We've known each other a little while now, Anna, and you appear to be a trustworthy person," he said. "So I'm going to let you look at these."

"What are they?" I leaned forward to touch the spine of one of the vintage-looking books.

"They're journals. This one's mine..." He picked up the brown leather-bound book. "This one's Meg's, and this one's Lexy's."

"How did you get hers?"

He leaned back and sighed. "Lexy was an orphan. She was raised by a wealthy old woman who had a large house out on Port Hogan Road."

"Okay." I was thinking of the document I'd seen when I was searching for Julian's birth certificate, but I couldn't make the connection.

"Miss Stella was what we all called her. Her name was Stella Walker. She was originally from North County, around Lake Pinette. Her husband died young, and she liked to foster children from the Little Flower Convent in Sterling. Until the child was adopted or moved to a different situation."

"What does that have to do with you having Ms. LaSalle's journal?"

"When Miss Stella died, she left her home to Lexy. Lexy wanted me to sell it so she could get something smaller." He paused. "I didn't exactly do that."

Now it all came together. "You bought it!"

"I'd intended to hold it as an investment property. But I never seemed to be able to part with it."

"You still own it?"

"Yes. And I was cleaning it out a while back and found this in one of the rooms. I did read it, and it was very... helpful to me."

"So you're going to let me read these?"

"Only for your information. Not for print, not for sharing with anyone."

"Why?" I cleared my throat. "I mean, why me?"

He stood and walked around the desk, leaning near me. "It'll help you understand why you need to trust us. Why you need to keep what you know a secret."

"I don't think anything could convince me that not telling Julian is for the best. He deserves to know you're his dad."

He looked down at his hands. "Julian has everything he needs. I have always taken good care of them, and I always will."

"But he needs a father," I argued. "He needs to know who you are."

"Lex is probably right. And once you read this, you'll understand her reasons." His voice was quiet, and I could tell this saddened him.

Still, I was amazed by what he was offering me, and I was itching to pick up the volumes and begin reading them at once.

"Can you agree to keep quiet if I give you these?" he asked.

"Yes. I've already said I wouldn't say anything."

"Be careful with them. It isn't just two people who could be hurt here." He stood and put the three books in my hands, and I felt like I'd just been entrusted with valuable artifacts.

I stood completely amazed, holding the books and almost a little frightened of what I might discover inside the yellowed pages.

"Anna?" He called.

I stopped and looked back. "Yes, sir?"

"I do want to know Julian as my son. Someday."

* * *

Mom was in the kitchen when I ran in, stopped at the door to hang my keys on the rack, and started to run up the stairs. I'd stuffed the journals in my book bag, and I had to hold it close to me because the top was gaping open with the additional load.

"Tough day at the office?" Mom smiled as she lifted the lid on the slow-cooker and gave something that smelled delicious a stab. I paused at the stairs.

"Oh, 'bout the same as always."

"Any news to share? Something not fit to print maybe?"

If she only knew! "Nothing I can spill just yet."

"Hey, come here for a sec." I sighed and put my bag on the stairs before trudging back to the kitchen.

"Don't act like that," she complained. "Listen, I know we've been sort of zooming past each other these last few weeks…"

"It's okay, Mom, Christmas on the Coast is a lot of work. I know." Every year she was consumed with the association's biggest fundraiser.

"But I was going to say, it's been a few months, and I noticed someone sort of dropped out of the picture."

Ugh. "Jack and I broke up," I said. And without warning, my silly eyes actually started filling with tears. I stepped back and pushed them away, clearing my throat. "I didn't tell you because it wasn't really a big deal."

Mom just looked at me frowning.

"Don't stare at me like that," I said trying to get control. "It really wasn't a big deal. We only went on one date." It was true. And she didn't need to know about all our other encounters.

"It just seemed like you liked him a lot. I saw the way you guys looked at each other."

My eyes closed, and I fought against the pain flaring in my chest. "Please don't make it seem like a bigger deal than it was."

I leaned back against the counter and sighed. Why did my emotions choose now to flood to the surface?

Mom was quiet a moment and then leaned next to me. "But he was kind of your first love, wasn't he?"

"No. What does that even mean? First love. That's so dumb. People say that, but it's not true. Weren't there any little boys in elementary school I thought I loved?"

"Oh, sure. That little Anthony kid who wore glasses and picked his nose. I remember you drawing pictures of the two of you getting married. He was definitely your first love."

I rolled my eyes.

"I'm just saying," she continued, "feel bad for as long as you need to, but don't act like it didn't happen."

"I'm not acting like it didn't happen."

"Well, I hope you don't feel like you have to hide this stuff from me."

We were still leaning against the counter, and I was staring at my shoes. "It just makes it worse when I tell people," I said. "Like sympathy makes me want to cry more or something."

Mom wrapped an arm around my shoulders and kissed my head. "Okay, well, I hear you. Just know I *am* sympathetic, but I won't make a big deal out of it."

"Thanks, Mom."

"But if you change your mind, and you want to make a big deal out of it, that's okay, too."

I nodded. "Deal."

"So the ultimate comfort food — I made beef stew for dinner!"

After dinner, I pulled the journals from under my bed. The first one I opened was the pink fabric-covered one that had belonged to Jack's mom. Her handwriting was all curly and cute, and the first words she'd written were her name in all its different forms across the page: *Margaret Louise Kyser, Mrs. William Kyser, Bill and Meg...*

I stopped and looked up, thinking of Rachel and Brad. Since the invention of the small-town high school, it seemed girls had been deciding their future husbands by graduation time. I flipped through the pages. There was stuff in here about Brad's parents, too...

Just then I heard a knock on my door and hastily shoved the books under my bed. Mom peeked her head in my room.

"Hey, honey. I'm turning in. You staying up late?"

"Not too late. I was just catching up on some reading."

She walked over to my desk and picked up the brown package that was still wrapped.

"What's this? A gift?"

I got up. "Oh, wow. I forgot. It's a Christmas gift from Lucy Kyser. I probably should get her something in return."

"You haven't opened it."

I picked up the package and hastily tore off the paper. My heart stopped when I saw what it was. In a beautiful antique-wood frame was a picture she'd snapped of Jack and me at that first school dance. I couldn't stop it now. Seeing his gorgeous smile and my blissful expression, remembering that night, kissing him on the beach, my palms against his warm chest, all of it, the tears streamed down my cheeks in a flood.

"Oh, Mom, I think I did love him," I whispered.

She helped me to my bed and rubbed my back as I dissolved into tears on my pillow.

Chapter 27

Every winter along the coast, an unseasonably warm, humid day would pop up right around Christmas. Sometimes a string of them. The next morning was one of those days.

The sky was white and dark grey, and the clouds were building into what looked like a strong storm. The idea of rain was perfect for what was going on in my chest, and I wanted to get out into the turbulent air and feel it on my face.

I scribbled out a note letting Mom know I was headed to the beach, I had my phone, and then I ran out to the car. The wind was pushing through in short, powerful bursts, and I couldn't wait to be out in it. I wanted sit on the shore and let go all of my feelings. I wanted to turn over the leaves of the past six months and try to understand what had happened to me, how I'd changed, and how I'd gotten off course. I wanted to let the noise of the surf pound out the bad and help me find my way back to the beginning, back to how I was before.

I arrived at the beach. Alone again. I remembered that fateful day last August, but this time I wasn't hiding. I was at a familiar stretch of public beach, and I went down to the shoreline to sit and watch the grey clouds roll in as the wind continued pushing my hair back and around my head. Two red flags today; water closed to the public.

A few local surfers made their way out to the waves that were growing in height as the storm approached. No lifeguard was on duty, but these kids had grown up taking chances on the water. It wouldn't be a bad storm, just enough to blow in some big waves and a strong shower or two. I closed my eyes and felt the salty blast against my cheeks.

Maybe I wouldn't go all the way back to the beginning. I wasn't sure I could even if I tried, but I had to go back to when I was stronger, when I had goals and I was focused on my career plan. SAT scores were in, and in a few months, I'd know for certain where I was going to college next year. All that was left were these last few months, prom, and graduation. The best parts of senior year, and for some, the best days of their lives.

I thought about that conversation with Gabi about what I wanted, and the decisions I'd made about having value and being the reason for someone.

When I opened my eyes again, there he stood. As if somehow he'd heard my thoughts and come here to find me. I shook my head. That wasn't right. He was holding a surfboard.

Julian looked out at the water several minutes then he glanced down and bent his knees to squat beside me on the sand. As always, his presence soothed me, almost making the bad stuff disappear. Almost bringing me all the way back to happy. It felt so close with him here.

"Waiting for someone?" he said.

I shook my head. "I just love when the weather's like this."

"Me, too. Great day to hang ten."

"I don't surf."

"I'm still waiting to teach you."

I studied his face and considered for a few seconds how much of a mistake it would be to take his hand and venture out into the swirling water. Letting him teach me to ride the waves that were growing in height, following him into the currents most people feared. I was a pretty good swimmer, and I trusted Julian.

"Okay," I said.

He pulled me up. "Let's go."

* * *

If you enjoyed this book by this author, please consider leaving a review at **Amazon, Barnes & Noble,** or **Goodreads**!

* * *

Be the first to know about New Releases by Leigh Talbert Moore! **Sign up for the New Release Mailing list today** at http://eepurl.com/tzVuP.

* * *

Undertow, Book 2 in the Dragonfly series, **coming July 2013!**

Undertow
by Leigh Talbert Moore

Recovering from her broken heart, Anna decides to spend the semester break diving into the three journals Bill Kyser gave her to read — the journals that hold the secret and that Bill says will help her understand his need for silence.

But the more Anna learns about the tragic events behind the powerful developer's seclusion, the more she's convinced silence is a mistake.

As her feelings for Julian grow deeper, Anna has to decide if she'll keep the secrets or tell him the truth about a past that's been buried for decades. The only problem is the more she knows, the more Anna realizes either choice could cost her the boy she loves.

Acknowledgments

In early 2010, when I finished the very first draft of *Dragonfly*, my very first novel, I timidly showed it to four people—my husband, Richard, and my friends Melissa Ott, Kim Barnes, and Allyson Johnson. And though it was very much "in the rough," not one of them said, "Don't quit your day job!" I'm so thankful for their early encouragement, and I have to thank them first for never letting me give up on my dream.

Thank you to my reader-friends, who make this job so much fun! I love hearing from you, reading your reviews, getting your tweets, seeing your emails and Facebook posts, thinking about your feedback, and most of all, meeting your demand for more! I wish I could sit down and thank each of you in person. You've given me such a gift to be able to do this full time.

Thank you to my precious daughters and my mom and dad, who hardly complain when I'm under tight deadlines, not keeping in touch very well, or generally stressed out. Thanks for putting up with a slightly messy house and somewhat distracted me. I love you guys so much.

Thank you to my writer-friends, who helped me go back and get this, my very first book, to a place where readers might enjoy meeting these characters and starting this journey. Thank you for always being supportive and generously sharing so much great advice. I wouldn't be here without you!

Thank you specifically to my cousin Odessa Toma, Susan Quinn, Tami Hart Johnson, Magan Vernon, Jolene Perry, Sharon Hattenstein, and Tracy Womack, who read and gave feedback. Thanks to Jolene Perry for her sailing wisdom and gorgeous cover design. Thanks to Allie Brennan for design support and writerly encouragement. Thanks to all my book club ladies for being so excited about cover images and pictures and quotes. And for not forgetting me 850 miles away — I love you guys!

Special thanks to Scott Montgomery and Jim Bleeke for helping me mentally and logistically after Richard's accident.

And thanks to God for giving me this storytelling gift, blessing me with the ability, and finding the readers who allow me do it full-time. Here's to all ten on the shelves, the first of which is Yours, opened doors, and touched so many hearts.

About the Author

Leigh Talbert Moore is a wife and mom by day, a writer by day, a reader by day, a former journalist, a former editor, a chocoholic, a caffeine addict, a lover of great love stories, a beach bum, and occasionally she sleeps.

Also by Leigh Talbert Moore:

The Truth About Faking (2012)
Rouge (2012)
The Truth About Letting Go (2013)

All of Leigh's books are available on Amazon, Barnes & Noble, iTunes, and Kobo.

Connect with Leigh online:

Blog: http://leightmoore.blogspot.com
Facebook: http://www.facebook.com/LeighTalbertMoore
Amazon Author page: amazon.com/author/leightmoore
Goodreads: http://www.goodreads.com/leightmoore
Twitter: https://twitter.com/leightmoore
Tumblr: http://leightmoore.tumblr.com

CPSIA information can be obtained
at www.ICGtesting.com
Printed in the USA
FSOW01n2120230317
32277FS